RHAPSODY IN BLACK

Borgo Press Fiction by BRIAN STABLEFORD

Alien Abduction: The Wiltshire Revelations
The Best of Both Worlds and Other Ambiguous Tales
Beyond the Colors of Darkness and Other Exotica
Changelings and Other Metaphoric Tales
Complications and Other Stories
The Cosmic Perspective and Other Black Comedies
The Cure for Love and Other Tales of the Biotech Revolution
The Dragon Man: A Novel of the Future
The Eleventh Hour
Firefly: A Novel of the Far Future
Les Fleurs du Mal: A Tale of the Biotech Revolution
The Gardens of Tantalus and Other Delusions
*The Great Chain of Being and Other Tales of the Biotech
    Revolution*
Halycon Drift (Hooded Swan #1)
The Haunted Bookshop and Other Apparitions
In the Flesh and Other Tales of the Biotech Revolution
The Innsmouth Heritage and Other Sequels
Kiss the Goat
Luscinia: A Romance of Nightingales and Roses
The Mad Trist: A Romance of Bibliomania
The Moment of Truth: A Novel of the Future
An Oasis of Horror: Decadent Tales and Contes Cruels
The Plurality of Worlds: A Sixteenth-Century Space Opera
Prelude to Eternity: A Romance of the First Time Machine
Promised Land (Hooded Swan #3)
The Quintessence of August: A Romance of Possession
The Return of the Djinn and Other Black Melodramas
Rhapsody in Black (Hooded Swan #2)
Salome and Other Decadent Fantasies
The Tree of Life and Other Tales of the Biotech Revolution
The Undead: A Tale of the Biotech Revolution
Valdemar's Daughter: A Romance of Mesmerism
*The World Beyond: A Sequel to S. Fowler Wright's The World
    Below*
Xeno's Paradox: A Tale of the Biotech Revolution
Zombies Don't Cry: A Tale of the Biotech Revolution

RHAPSODY IN BLACK

HOODED SWAN, BOOK TWO

BRIAN STABLEFORD

THE BORGO PRESS
MMXI

RHAPSODY IN BLACK

FIRST BORGO PRESS EDITION

Published by Wildside Press LLC

www.wildsidebooks.com

DEDICATION

For Jack Spratling

CONTENTS

PROLOGUE 9

CHAPTER ONE 13

CHAPTER TWO. 29

CHAPTER THREE 41

CHAPTER FOUR 47

CHAPTER FIVE. 55

CHAPTER SIX. 65

CHAPTER SEVEN 79

CHAPTER EIGHT 87

CHAPTER NINE 95

CHAPTER TEN 101

CHAPTER ELEVEN. 111

CHAPTER TWELVE 119

CHAPTER THIRTEEN 133

CHAPTER FOURTEEN 145

CHAPTER FIFTEEN 155

CHAPTER SIXTEEN 169

CHAPTER SEVENTEEN 173

ABOUT THE AUTHOR 179

PROLOGUE

I spent two long years on a bleak world circling a cold sun on the edge of the Halcyon Drift. I was lucky. There was air, and water, and the local vegetation was digestible enough to keep me alive—just. I was also unlucky. My ship was smashed and my partner was dead and even with a bleep sending out a perpetual cry for help the situation had a hint of the hopeless about it. Those two years did me more harm than the half-a-lifetime I had spent in space. A spaceman's expectancy of life is not so grand that two years can go missing and not matter.

I had little to occupy my time on the rock except survival and standing up the cross on Lapthorn's grave every time the wind blew it down—which was often. I had memories, but I'm not a man to derive much warmth from memories, and they were more like ghosts that haunted me.

Ultimately, the wind began to talk to me. I listened. I was picked up by a ramrod which was searching for the legendary *Lost Star* and had homed in on the wrong bleep. The wind still talked to me—I had picked up a parasite, and acquired a companion for all time. I didn't like him (I thought of it as 'him'). He took some getting used to.

I felt bad enough after two years on the rock (I called it Lapthorn's Grave) but the Caradoc Company, who owned the ramrod which lifted me, were intent on making things worse. They claimed a salvage fee. The court sided with them, and before I knew where I was I'd been dumped on Earth with a debt of twenty thousand hanging over the rest of my life like the

Sword of Damocles. It's a hard life.

I went to look up some people. The man who'd taught me to fly was dead. All that remained of my distant past was an empty workshop and Herault's grandson. Lapthorn's family were alive and well and interested, but I wanted nothing to do with them. I'd had my fill of ghosts and I wanted to forget poor Lapthorn. Even that was not to be. I had to get work, and the only work that was offered to me was a job flying the *Hooded Swan* for a New Alexandrian scientist/politician named Titus Charlot. The job was worth twenty thousand over two years but the contract I signed virtually sold my soul to Charlot. Charlot figured himself as puppet-master to the galaxy—alien races as welt as human. I didn't see it that way, and neither did the galaxy. I knew as soon as I saw him that I was in for a rough spell.

The *Swan* was a great ship—the best—but her crew was makeshift. In the beginning she had a good engineer in Rothgar, but he soon figured out what was what and quit like a sensible man. The ones who stayed were all people I'd rather not have had around. Nick delArco was the captain—he'd built the ship and he was a very pleasant and gentle man, but he wasn't competent to take charge of a perambulator. Eve Lapthorn was reserve pilot. Johnny Socoro—Herault's grandson—was reserve engineer, and he got quick promotion, which made him big-headed as well as hot-headed.

Job number one was a crazy jaunt in pursuit of the good old legendary *Lost Star* bleep. It was a fashionable way of committing suicide just then. We won the race for our little-loved but much-respected owner, but nobody reaped much of a harvest from the affair. People got killed, including a friend of mine named Alachakh. People do get killed, I know, but I'm not a violent man and I don't like to be around when it happens. The better I got to know Charlot the better I understood the fact that I was liable to be around when some more people got killed. The Companies, including Caradoc, were expanding at a phenomenal rate, and the commercial subjugation of the galaxy was well under way. New Alexandria and New Rome were the only forces trying to keep the lid on, and I was just one of the recruits to their cause. I didn't know how long the balance of power would stay balanced, but I knew I didn't want to be around when it tipped. Trouble and strife were on the way, and I didn't like the prospect of being a pawn in the game.

I handled the *Lost Star* affair brilliantly. But that was only the beginning.

CHAPTER ONE

Calm down, urged the whisper.

I stopped, breathing heavily, to take stock of myself and of the situation. I was ankle-deep in cold, slimy water, and my flashlight was noticeably weaker. Perhaps I had every right to a touch of panic in my movements, but the wind obviously thought that I was overdoing it.

You can't go much farther at this pace, he said. You'll drive yourself to prostration. And there's no point. They gave up chasing you twenty minutes ago. They've got better sense than to lose themselves down here.

He was only trying to be helpful. In his fashion, he was always trying to be helpful. I found his eternal vigilance and limitless fount of common sense to be overly patronising and rather irritating. I had not yet conceded him the right to be as concerned for my welfare as I was, despite the fact that he had a similarly considerable stake in it. (But there was one important difference, of course. He could always find new lodgings if his present slum was condemned. I couldn't.)

'This light,' I told him, 'is going to go out before we've covered many more miles.'

So? The locals don't carry flashlights. They manage in the dark.

'All very well if you know where you're going, and have been walking blindfold around these caves since you were two years old.'

You're not afraid of the dark, are you?

'Yes.'

In that case, why did you ever start out on this idiot's crusade?

'You know damn well. You were there, remember? I didn't start the thing. I didn't want any part of it. It was Sampson and Johnny.'

They didn't force you to leave your comfortable jail cell.

'No, but with the door standing open like that, squatting in the cage till doomsday suddenly seemed to be a most unattractive prospect'

And so you ran. Well now, here you are. On the run and soon to be in the dark. We can go back, you know, and ask them to lock you up again. If that's what you want, decide now and turn round. If that's not what you want, then start thinking about where we're going, and why.

'At this moment,' I said, 'I'm not in a very good spot for sitting down to work out a strategy. Besides which, I'm in the dark in more ways than one.'

To this, he made no verbal reply. He held his peace, allowing me to go the way of my choice without further delay. I could sense neither approval nor disapproval when I went forward again. In all probability, he couldn't make up his mind what he wanted us to do either.

I stumbled on along the tunnel. My right hand balanced me against the wall which I was following, while the left held the flashlight, swinging it in steady arcs to show me as much as possible of the way I had chosen to go. There was just black water and black stone, but it meant a lot just to be able to see it. The tunnel was wide here, and a comfortable height, and the flash couldn't do a very efficient job of highlighting the far wall. There was a circular yellow blur, and that was all.

I tried to run, but running through shallow water is just not practicable where any sort of distance is involved, and I had to settle for slow, purposeful wading. But I still concentrated all my effort on progress, and spared no part of my mind for contemplating destinations.

We can't just run, said the whisper, trying to prompt me. Not in a place like this. You can run until you drop, and still be nowhere. You've got to have some kind of a pattern in mind. You've got to decide the sort of hand you're trying to play. It's not enough simply to be down here. We have to have a reason. Now you're here, you have to try to cut yourself some kind of slice of the action. It's not enough just to wander around and get lost. There must be thousands of miles of cave and shaft in this honeycomb. You could die and your bones need never be discovered. You've got to have *something* in your mind.

'I have,' I said. 'You.'

This is no time for indulging your ridiculous sense of humour.

'On the contrary. This is exactly the sort of time to which my sense of humour is tailored'

Be reasonable!

There should have been a thousand reasons why the wind and I were incompatible. But that was the only one that really bugged *him*.

'Look,' I said. 'For the time being, there's only one way to go. We're in a tunnel, right? When I get offered alternatives, that's the time I begin making choices. And even then it won't be too difficult. I don't want to be any farther up, because it's too damn cold where I am. Ergo I want to go down. And, if I remember correctly, the way to navigate to the lower strata of an alveolar system is to follow the current of cold air.'

You don't know anything about navigation in alveolar systems.

'I know enough of the jargon to provide excuses for anything I choose to do. And I know that hot air rises and cold air falls. That's all that's relevant at present.'

It's not as simple as that, he said darkly.

I was slowing down. The water was creeping up my calves. The bitter cold was numbing my feet and sending shooting pains up my legs. The hand which I was using to support myself was suffering, too. Except where it was encrusted with lichenous growths, the rock was like sandpaper. It spoke well for the constancy and stability of the system that the water had never come up far enough to erode the surface smooth, but it was hell on my fingertips. The cold was beginning to soak into my insides, as well. I'd had to come up rather than going down in order to avoid the initial pursuit. Being linked to the surface lock, the reception area where we'd been imprisoned was above the capital and the highways. Hence, to go down would be to play into the hands of the enemy. But I'd shaken off the nasties some time back, and I'd covered enough sideways ground to be fairly certain that I wouldn't drop back into the streets of the capital.

The problem was what to do when I did get back down to the inhabited strata. Before the breakout, Johnny had been rambling about some vague and ridiculous scheme to steal surface suits and win our way back to the *Hooded Swan*. No doubt he had some even vaguer idea of mustering the *Swan*'s considerable artillery and taking the entire world by force. But the whole thing was a joke. There was no chance whatsoever of reaching the *Swan*. That was one hole the miners would have well and truly stoppered.

Ergo, I had to play a different sort of hand altogether. I had to do whatever I was going to do down here, in the caves. And the obvious immediate aim was to find out what the hell was going on. This endless secrecy was getting on my nerves. At least two people—Charlot and Sampson—knew more than they were letting on, or they wouldn't be here. I was grossly offended by the fact that they staunchly refused to let me in on their idiot schemes. Although I didn't actually make any sort of firm resolution, I already had it in the back of my mind to do my level best to make a thorough mess of any plans either of them might have.

The first step in working my way back into the pattern of events seemed to necessitate making new contacts in the Rhapsody culture. The miners seemed to have suddenly become the police force, so that let them out. The Hierarchy of the Church I wouldn't approach in an asbestos suit. But even considering the paucity of opportunity on Rhapsody, that still left a goodly proportion of the population which might be approachable and where I might be able to find friends.

It was not going to be easy, though. I knew virtually nothing about the culture beyond my contempt for its *raison d'être*. My prospects seemed very dubious indeed.

'It *would* have been a great deal simpler not to get involved in this mess at all,' I conceded.

Too late now, he said.

'In fact,' I went on, 'it would have been even simpler to have stayed at home. The further this contract with Charlot goes, the more trouble I get into. At this rate, the odds against my surviving the two years look somewhat considerable.'

This is your mess, said the wind. You can't blame Charlot for this.

'I can and I do,' I replied, perversely. 'If it wasn't for him, I'd likely be on Penaflor, in a nice, safe job.'

Working for nothing, the rest of your life.

'True, but there'd be a lot of the rest of my life. With Charlot, I'm not so sure.'

This is just wasted effort, said the whisper. Regret is a waste of time. Keep your mind on the issue at hand.

The tunnel curved to the left, and I felt the water speed up abruptly as it flowed around my legs. I knew there had to be an imminent declivity, and I tested the rock carefully with my boot. The water was uncomfortably fast, and I had to stand carefully to avoid being dragged from my feet. I had no wish to try swimming in the stream.

The flashlight showed me the drop, and it didn't seem to slope so steeply as to be unnegotiable. But visibility was only a few metres.

'The principle of Let Well Alone,' I said idly, while I contemplated the prospect, 'is unusually good sense, to say that it came out of New Rome. If Titus Charlot had the sense to follow the principle, we wouldn't be in this mess. Let Well Alone isn't ethics or diplomacy, you know. It's simple self-protection.'

A breach of the principle isn't against the law, said the wind, drawn into the argument against his will. You can't sue him for it.

'Pity.'

I began picking my way down the slope. Very slowly. Very carefully.

The water dwindled from my calves to my ankles again, but it was no less treacherous for that. I hugged the wall as close as I could, and I had to use my left arm for balancing purposes, which meant that when I wanted to use the flash, I had to stop.

In the meantime, my thoughts rambled on.

'If I ever take a Christian name,' I said, 'I think Job would suit me best. Job with the built-in comforter. Very apt. Poetic justice, even. You have no real appreciation for the sadness of my situation. How any parasite of mine could possibly take Charlot's part against me is quite beyond me. It smacks of disloyalty and a total lack of sympathy.'

Are you getting hysterical? he asked.

'Don't be ridiculous. I have never been hysterical in my life. I am merely indulging my twisted sense of humour, in order to keep my mind from direr thoughts, such as the possibility of slipping, and what might happen to me if I do. It is quite deliberate, conscious and controlled, I've lived in this body a lot longer than you have, and I wish you'd let me handle it in the manner to which it is accustomed rather than the manner to which you'd like it to become accustomed. You cannot teach old bodies new tricks. If you're going to live here, you'd better get used to the intellectual climate. We never have storms, but it isn't a South Sea vacation paradise, for all that. Worry not, old friend. If this hill ever comes to sane, safe ground again, then I shall be off once again in pursuit of the plan which has burst from my head like Athene, in full armour—a stroke of genuine inspiration.'

What plan? he interrupted.

I didn't like being interrupted. It wasn't safe.

'To play by ear, of course,' I told him. 'To take each moment as it comes, and to follow my feelings. To do as I see fit, at each and every juncture, and not to concern myself with how each action might fit into the grandiose plans of fate and fortune. I always have bad luck anyway. *Ah!* I apologise most sincerely to fate and fortune both. I'll never say a bad word about them again.'

I'd found a ledge. Gratefully, I stepped out of the water. The ledge ran along the right-hand wall, and was just wide enough to accommodate me. The tunnel still sloped downward, though, and quite steeply. A few feet away, there was a crevice in the rock which wandered away at right angles to the lateral direction in which I was travelling. Had it been an upright passage, I might have followed it, but it slanted at fifty degrees or less from the horizontal, and looked even less comfortable than my present course. So I went on.

The wind seemed relieved that I'd broken off my uneasy monologue, and I suspected that he wanted to start up a more satisfactory (from his point of view) conversation, but couldn't think of anything appropriate to say.

It was not often that he was tongue-tied, and I wasn't sorry to get an extra moment's rest from him. I suppose that some people might consider it a great convenience to be sharing their skull with another mind, on the grounds that two points of view are better than one. They might even consider it to be especially convenient that the alien mind couldn't stay alien, but had to organise itself along lines similar to their own—become human, in fact. It means, after all, that one need never be alone. It means that one never need be completely isolated from one's own kind. It means the everpresence of a friend, which might be necessary in times of dire need—such as when I blacked out at a most inconvenient moment in a hyoplasmic lesion surrounding a star in the Halcyon Drift. It means an extra force with which to oppose the slings and arrows of outrageous fortune and illimitable seas of troubles, and an extra chance to end such troubles.

But as well as all that, it is also a bloody nuisance. There are times when one requires total peace, not simply as a concession on the part of a companion but as a private slice of one's own existence. And that was what I didn't have. Not any more. And since disadvantages are always more irritating than advantages are soothing, I was distinctly unappreciative of the alien commensalism. (I say commensalism because he claimed to be a *symbiote*, not a parasite.) He understood, and he wasn't bitter about it, or overly impatient. After all, compatibility was very much in his interests. Indeed, it was *his* way of life. My way of life, previously, had consisted of wilful isolation, and even alienation. I was a loner, a confirmed outsider. It was difficult adjusting to the enforced change, but there was no point in resisting it. I couldn't get rid of the whisper. No way. We were together until death us did part. I couldn't afford to hate him, but I couldn't help resenting him. We weren't ever going to be soulmates.

It is, as many philosophers have observed, a hard life.

As the ledge narrowed, I was forced to stand sideways, with my heels to the wall, in order to move along it. The flashlight was now useless and I was forced to *feel* my way along the passage by fluttering my right hand over the surface of the rock face. I dared not lift up my feet but slid them along the ledge. As I progressed, the floor beneath the ledge, along which the stream ran, began to fall away at a much steeper angle. The water became noisy as it rushed down the declivity, perhaps ultimately to fall into a vertical pit. Once I was certain that to fall off the ledge meant death, I lost interest in the precise geometry of the watercourse.

Suddenly, my right hand encountered empty space, and I stopped dead. There was no question of reassuring subvocal patter now. I was frightened. I drew back my hand and blew on the cold-numbed, flesh-stripped fingertips to make sure that they were still adequately sensitive to touch, and then sent them scuttling along the rock.

I discovered the edge, and found that it was not simply a bend, but a hairpin reverse. The rock at my back was a wedge of what seemed to me then to be fragile thinness. Almost reflexively, I pulled myself erect, so that I did not lean on it so heavily. I inched forward, hoping that the ledge would not give out. As I reached the ultimate projection of the rock face, I shut my eyes—I could see nothing in any case, with the flashlight pressed to the rock behind me—and pushed my foot slowly around the corner, toe down.

In my mind's eye, I could see myself balanced on the end of a chisel-shaped spur of rock projecting into nowhere, with an immeasurable abyss beneath me. The susurrus of running water now contained an ominous gurgle which suggested abysmal depths to my sensitive imagination.

Then my toe found a floor. It might only be a ledge as narrow as the one on which I was now standing, but I dared not contort my leg any further in order to explore its whole extent. The simple fact that a way out *did* exist was enough for me at that moment.

I had to turn round in order to negotiate the corner, and that offered difficulties. I transferred the flashlight from left hand to right, but decided it would be no more convenient there. I couldn't stick it in my belt, where it would get in between me and the wall. It was too big to hold sideways in my mouth, as pirates were once reputed to have carried cutlasses. I came to the conclusion that the only place it would be out of harm's way, and also in no danger of being lost, was dropped down the neck of my shirt at the back. This, of course, meant that I would be denied its light. Not that the light would be particularly useful, but it was a comforting thing to have around.

However, when needs must...

Turning myself face in to the rock wasn't too difficult. The wall was almost plumb vertical, fortunately. Had it leaned towards me, I would very likely have lost my balance and fallen.

Once my body was correctly orientated, I began to curl myself around the chisel-head, with my arms at full stretch on either side of the hairpin, and my feet as close together as I dared put them without endangering my equilibrium. It took me only a few seconds to ooze my body around the corner, but they were precarious seconds, and living them was by no means easy.

When I had recovered myself fully, I began to explore with my toe again, sending my left foot out cautiously to investigate the width of rock available to me.

There was an awful lot of it.

I turned around where I stood, luxuriating in the space which made the manoeuvre comfortable, and then fished the flashlight out of the small of my back—a feat almost as difficult as rounding the corner.

When I switched it on, I saw that although the *wall* turned through an angle of about one-sixty-five degrees, the *floor* only turned through eighty or so. There was another wall some six or seven feet away.

'Bloody hell!' I said with feeling. It had been a lot easier than I'd thought.

Caution never did anyone any harm, said the wind, comfortingly.

'Go to hell,' I said. Then I began to walk along the tunnel, playing the light along the floor in front of me. It wasn't so cold, either, though I was still walking down the airstream. The current was slower, here, though. I didn't know nearly enough about the aerodynamics of alveolar strata to judge exactly what that meant. It was presumably a venous shaft rather than an arterial, but whether the strength of the current was determined by the architecture of this element in the system, or by the connections it made with other tunnels, I couldn't say. Probably both.

I could hear the faint rustle of water behind the walls, and that too would have its part to play in maintaining the local temperature clines which determined the precise pattern of the airflow. The water itself was recycled by evaporation and dispersion throughout the infundibular hotshafts which dropped all the way from the summit of the alveolar rock-tissue to the surface of the hotcore.

I began to move quickly again, now that it was easy. There was no sense in dawdling—I was still chilled, and I would have to find warmer air than this in order to thaw out properly.

At first, the tunnel was high and wide, and might have been tailored. But there was no sign of stoneworking. I wondered whether there was some obliging principle of physics which determined that the optimum tube dimensions in alveolar rock were just about right for accommodating people. Or, conversely, there might be some ironic principle of the life sciences which determined that humans should grow to a convenient size for the troglodytic existence, rather than the star-conquering existence which many of them seemed to prefer (or at least aspire to).

In actual fact, it was only the fact that these honeycombs seemed to have been designed with man in mind that enabled worlds like this one to be colonised. A system like this one could take only so much knocking about. Once the architecture was altered beyond a certain point, extreme changes could take place in the air-and-water circulation patterns, with potentially disastrous consequences for cultures whose livelihood depended on things staying the way they were. Some highly civilised worlds of this type had the science and the scientists to determine exactly what they could and couldn't do to a warren. Some could even alter warrens in order to make the air and water do what they wanted. But Rhapsody wasn't a highly civilised world. It was a galactic slum—a religious alienist culture with a high regard for hardship and none for efficiency or safety.

So where are we going? the wind wanted to know. It's all very well to play by ear and make up the plan of action as you go along. But we have to start somewhere. So where?

'Well,' I said, 'we have to eat. To find food we find people. This offers us a choice between the shanty towns which are undoubtedly sprinkled around this big Swiss cheese and the mine-faces and conversion plants at which the world earns its collective living.

'Now, as we have already observed, the miners have decided that they have a crucial part to play in this silly drama, and that part involves waving guns around. Assuming that the conversion plants, as the lifeblood of the culture, are protected from all forms of social irresponsibility, I therefore conclude that if we are going to eke out a temporary existence as a thief and a vagabond, the place to do it is the townships. Fair enough?'

He didn't say anything, so he was obviously satisfied for the time being with my declared intentions. When I was going well, he was always content to leave me to it. He didn't argue for the sake of it, as I was occasionally prone to do. I am a confirmed opponent. Say something, and I'll disagree with it. On principle. And while I might not know what the hell I am talking about, I am occasionally disposed to defend it with considerable passion and obstinacy.

We all have our faults.

The corridor funnelled into a capillary, and I was forced to crawl. The passage seemed to be an unduloid rather than a cylinder, which meant that on occasion I had to lay myself out snake-fashion and work my way through bottlenecks, whereas at other times I was permitted to employ a fast shamble in order to progress. The air current became stronger as the air was pressured through the irised collars of rock, and its coldness became a great inconvenience. No doubt, of course, I caused the air concomitant inconvenience as I acted as a considerable obstacle to its natural flow. I was extremely glad that it was a tailwind. To crawl the other way would have been well-nigh impossible. When I stretched myself through the bottlenecks, I felt like a dart in a blowpipe.

It wasn't a great way to travel.

'Worms must feel like this,' I said, half complaining, half sympathising with the lesser brethren of humankind.

The walls were slightly damp, and I occasionally came across patches of slime and grease that were undoubtedly protoplasmic. Despite the fact that alveolar systems lack the encouragement and assistance of solar radiation, they almost invariably contrive to evolve quite prolific life-systems. Because they are networks and not surfaces, and because a planet-wide stratum might contain hundreds, or even thousands, of unconnected warrens, the lifesystems tend to be incredibly diverse, and it is not unusual to find four or five separate evolutions in the one warren. The prospects of niche diversification are strictly limited, and unless the life-system is highly imaginative, it can rarely manage more than half a dozen different plasmid forms. Owing to the consequent lack of selective pressure, speciation tends to be very cursory, and divergent development tends to take place across boundaries which are solely defined by nutritional stratification. A life-system which might be regarded as 'typical', therefore, would probably consist of one 'plant' superorganism—a thermosynth, not a photosynth—one 'animal herbivore' type and one secondary consumer (often given a little assistance by a secondary thermosynthetic capability, and therefore unclassifiable as plant or animal). Plus, of course, the customary couple of parasites thrown in for the sake of that immortal ecological principle:

> Big bugs have little bugs
> Upon their backs to bite 'em,
> And little bugs have lesser bugs,
> And so *ad infinitum*.

Which is probably the only universal ecological rule.

Worms, contributed the wind, somewhat belatedly, have to eat out their own tunnels.

I hoped that this particular passage wouldn't get so narrow that it would take an excavator to get me through. But that was unlikely, bearing in mind the confidence of the air current. At the time, I was extremely thin, having been given no period of free time long enough to allow me to recuperate from my sojourn on Lapthorn's Grave, where I had been on the brink of starvation for two years.

And as it turned out, I was all right. The hole finally ducked into a sharp downslope and emerged into the ceiling of a much wider, taller tunnel. This one was engineered, if you can call beating your way through inconvenient outcrops with a pickaxe 'engineering'.

I had been an hour or more squirming my way through the slimy sheath before I achieved this outlet, but the rock had become noticeably warmer as I progressed, and although I had never contrived to be comfortable, I had begun to worry less about dying of exposure and more about skinning myself alive.

After I dropped from the bottleneck into the new corridor, I took the rest to which I'd been entitled for some time. I curled myself up into a seated foetal position, and switched out the flashlight, which was still heroically shining on, although still weakening inexorably.

There was no light—natural or artificial—in the tunnel. Neither was there a groove or a set of rails for vehicles to run along. This was highly unusual in an alveolar culture, and I presumed that the religious tenets on which the colony was founded included the assumption that God gave us legs for walking on. The passage was obviously a thoroughfare despite its lack of provision for transport. The evidence of stone-clearing was quite obvious, and nobody clears rock unless they intend putting the cleared passage to regular use. I reflected on the inconsistency of a society's being forced to employ sophisti-cated heat-powered food-producing conversion machines, with all the careful organic husbandry which that implied, yet at the same time denying itself even primitive—and cheap—wheeled transport systems. There's no accounting for the way people choose to exist.

The air in the corridor flowed from left to right as I sat with my back to the wall below the hole from which I had emerged. Unless my sense of direction had totally betrayed me, the capital lay to my left, and this was an afferent vessel. The air was a little too cool for my personal taste, and a lot colder than warren dwellers usually preferred, but I put that down to the world's personal eccentricities, and decided that it was not incompatible with the theory that this was a main road connecting the capital to a smaller township. The lack of traffic would also have argued against this hypothesis, except for the fact that there was some-thing like a national emergency and the normal routines would have been completely obliterated.

'I'm hungry,' I complained unenthusiastically. Complaint is an unimaginative seed for a conversation, but the wind seemed to have nothing to say, and I was becoming bored with sitting in silence. The alternative—the resumption of my wandering—did not immediately appeal to me, as I was still extremely fatigued.

You should have reminded your impulsive friends that jailbreaks are more conveniently situated after meals, said the wind morosely.

'You make the assumption, of course, that these religious maniacs were going to feed us pagans,' I pointed out.

Only the nastiest of societies fail to feed their guests.

'That's what I mean.'

If you could overcome your distaste for religious communities, I think you'd find that there are much worse people to have to deal with than the Church of the Exclusive Reward. You should know, after the years you spent trading on the lunatic fringe.

'The galactic rim.'

Call it what you will.

All this merry chit-chat, of course, wasn't getting us any place. But it was helping to reduce my burden of fatigue. To look at the world with a kindlier eye is to be no less a realist, but serves to make fearsome the possibilities of failure and doom.

I suppose that I could even become amenable to the hardness of my fortune, if it wasn't for the delight which Charlot took in keeping me firmly under his thumb. And also for the lunatic notions which he used as chessboards on which to push his pawns. Like recovering the *Lost Star* treasure from the heart of the Halcyon Drift.

And, in all likelihood, like the present jaunt.

Picking up Splinterdrift on Attalus, and giving them a free ride home....

CHAPTER TWO

I hated Attalus.

It was always foggy on Attalus.

I really don't know how they ever came to build a major spaceport on a world so blatantly useless. Certainly not in order that it should become a home from home for refugees from God's Nine Splinters.

Probably it was because Attalus's star was practically cheek to cheek with Fomalhaut. Because they were visible targets, early starships had a tendency to head for stars that looked bright and beautiful in the dilute skies of Mother Earth.

Colonies thus tended to spring up in such regions, even if said stars were no great shakes from the point of view of utility, and pretty run-of-the-mill by transgalactic standards. The first spacemen, of course, didn't *have* transgalactic standards, but that doesn't wholly explain a blithe disregard for economic convenience.

In any case, Attalus survived by virtue of long establishment and a little extra effort. And, by pure coincidence, it did happen to be rather close to the system where the Church of the Exclusive Reward established God's Nine Splinters. Even Attalus couldn't be described as convenient, because the Splintermen had deliberately tucked themselves out of the way, but it was near enough to be the jumping-off point for exiles, and the transit station for such ships as ever did go that way.

The Attalians accepted as a matter of course that they were the middlemen between the Splinters and Civilisation. As a trade route, it was virtually useless, but on worlds whose continued success is fairly fragile, everybody has to count the last cent and a half. Every little helps.

I was in a damp mood anyway, when I set the *Swan* down on Attalus field, and my state of mind grew progressively worse as I saw the fog, the port and the hotel, in that order. I'd been commanded out here without a word of explanation, and to make things twice as unbearable, Titus Charlot had come along in person. This was his private mission, and couldn't be trusted to agents and hirelings. Especially not after what had happened with regard to the *Lost Star.*

Charlot hadn't stopped seething yet over that little matter. It didn't show in his general conduct—especially not where Nick delArco and Eve were concerned—but I detected the occasional edge to his voice and glint in his eyes when he addressed himself to me.

Even at his best, he was never the life and soul of anybody's party. With that memory and its attendant suspicions still rankling in his brain, he was a real bastard. The others managed to get along with him, with the possible exception of Nick, who—as captain of the *Swan*—felt the heaviness of his presence on board rather more than Eve or Johnny. But I found his standing beside me while I rode the bird to be a considerable annoyance. He didn't care. He had no interest in owning a happy ship. He just wanted a crew that he could manipulate to his own ends, and one that he could be seen to manipulate. A vain man, was Titus Charlot.

I'd warned Eve and Nick and Johnny before we even lifted for Attalus that they'd be better off working for someone else. But no matter how much better off they might be out of it, they were hanging onto the *Hooded Swan*. It made sense, in its way. There wasn't yet another ship in the galaxy that was anything like her, and they were all as close to her, each in his/her own way, as I was.

Nick had built the *Hooded Swan*. He had got the contract to turn an idea and a set of drawings and a mound of computer printout into an entity of matter and energy, a living being with a soul. And then they had offered him another contract—this one to become her captain. How could he have refused? How could he back out?

And in her pretty belly, the *Swan* carried Johnny's first baby. His engine. His drive-unit. Rothgar had taught him how to feed it and fondle it and clean it and attend faithfully to its every need and whim, but now it was all his. He and he alone was pacemaker to the heart of the most beautiful ship that ever flew. He couldn't give it up. He wasn't Rothgar, to absorb the whole experience in one trip and then need no more of it for it to be with him forever. Johnny was only a boy. No experience, no rank. Apart from the *Hooded Swan*, he was a nothing. Wild horses, as they say, couldn't have dragged him away.

Eve's reasons were somewhat more subtle. Difficult to see and difficult to understand. There was something odd between Eve and her brother, despite the fact that she hadn't seen him since she was a child. When I'd brought home news of her brother's death, she'd transferred some part of that relationship to me. It was nothing so crude and vulgar as being in love with me. In a sense, it was as though I were Lapthorn's ghost. I was nothing like Michael Lapthorn, of course—we could hardly have been more different. But she didn't know that. To her, I was her brother's hero, her brother's partner- all that was left, in fact, of her brother. (In actual fact, she was much closer to being Lapthorn's ghost than I was. The facial similarity was no more than one would usually expect between siblings, but I could sense in her a weird echo of Lapthorn's *hunger*—his greed for experience and his insatiability.)

And Eve had an extra reason, above and beyond wanting to stick close to me. She too was a pilot. She had her own hood and her own electroplates stowed somewhere aboard the ship. She had ridden the bird—in atmosphere only—on her initial test series. She was enough of a pilot to know that I was a damn sight better one, but she was also enough of a pilot to love this ship, forsaking all others. Steering a flying tin can was no way to live once you'd actually felt the *Swan*'s wings in your fingers, and her heart inside your body.

So we were all stuck with the ship, for one reason or another. My reasons, of course, were simplest of all. Titus Charlot had legal title to a two-year lease on my soul. I was in no position to argue. Quite apart from that, the *Hooded Swan* was the best ship in existence. I was the best pilot. We deserved one another.

The four of us who were the crew on the *Swan* were mismatched, though. We had started out on a note of falseness and mistrust, but eventually we were forced into coexistence and mutual tolerance, so that wasn't the reason. I'm not quite sure what the real reason was. It could simply be that we were out of one another's contexts—that our personal interactions weren't aligned with our status aboard the ship. Nick delArco, for instance, was a nice guy, but he couldn't command a rowing boat. He was too soft and he knew next to nothing about deep space. He was a counterfeit captain, strings pulled courtesy of Titus Charlot. I had no beef with him whatsoever as an acquaintance or as a shipbuilder, but as an immediate boss, in between me and Charlot, he was an unnecessary embarrassment.

And so, for that matter, was Eve. I didn't want an understudy aboard any ship of mine, especially not one who thought I was the shade of her long-lost brother.

Johnny, I guess, would have been perfectly OK in any other crew. Nobody had anything against Johnny. But he tried too hard. He was always trying to push people the way he thought they ought to go. He reacted too hard. He admired delArco far too much, he was infatuated with Eve, and his picture of me was far too good to be true.

The whole set-up was a mess.

Charlot's intellectual speciality was mixing, blending, sorting, separating and using. He was a perfect New Alexandrian. We were as much his toys as were his computer programmes and his beloved syntheses of alien intellects.

My first thought, when we were ordered to Attalus, was that he had found some new toys to provide him with a temporary diversion. That impression seemed to be confirmed when the first thing he did, after landfall, was to search out the current head man among the exiles from God's Nine Splinters.

That man was Rion Mavra. Charlot introduced us to him, but didn't explain what he wanted with Splinterdrift. At that point, he probably hadn't explained to Mavra either. We also met several other examples of the Splinter culture at the same time, including Mavra's wife, Cyclide, and his cousin, Cyolus Capra. There was no hint of any warmness in any of the greetings. You'd think that the exiles would be grateful for someone seeking them out and talking to them. After all, they'd been kicked off their home world onto an under-populated, rather unpleasant world which might tolerate them, but certainly wouldn't make them welcome.

But the exiles remained cold and distant, trying to demonstrate that they were a considerable way above such considerations as loneliness. They seemed pleased to be able to withdraw from our company as soon as the formalities were over, but Charlot made arrangements to talk to them all again in the near future.

Then we went *our* way, to the hotel.

'Well,' said Charlot, as we walked through the fog-bound streets, 'what do you think of them?'

I think the remark was addressed to delArco, but Nick wasn't paying attention, so it was me who answered. 'What are we supposed to think? You haven't told us what's going on yet.'

He laughed gently. We reached the door of the hotel, and went through into the warmth and light. I was in urgent need of the customary shower and change of clothes after three days in the cradle, but Charlot obviously wanted to talk to us before going to his arranged meeting with Mavra and his companions. He ushered us into the lounge, and we seated ourselves around a low table. Nick ordered us some drinks.

'Rion Mavra comes from Rhapsody,' said Charlot.

'And that's where we're going?' asked Nick.

'That's right.' He turned to me. 'Have you ever been to the

Splinters?'

'No,' I replied. 'By all accounts they aren't worth a visit. Besides, the principle of Let Well Alone operates.'

'The principle of Let Well Alone doesn't operate,' said Charlot. 'It merely exists. A ridiculous institution.'

'It's worth taking notice of,' I told him. 'It isn't applied without reason.'

'It is applied purely and simply to help maintain the fiction that the Law of New Rome has some kind of universal validity and jurisdiction. Anywhere which refuses point-blank to pay even lip service to the Law is labelled "Let Well Alone", on the grounds that any citizen of the galaxy is beyond the protection of the Law on such a world. But you, of all people, should know how little protection the Law offers to anyone on any world outside the core. The principle of Let Well Alone is a tourist guide, nothing more.'

'Any world,' I said, 'which refuses to accept even the spirit of the Law of New Rome is *ipso facto* dangerous.'

'The Splinters reject everything which is offered to them or asked of them, by the galaxy. They're an isolationist group. But they're a religious community. Certainly not lawless.'

'It doesn't necessarily follow,' I persisted. Not that I really thought that Rhapsody was a hotbed of murder and rape, of course. I just didn't particularly want to go there.

Charlot knew I didn't have any real quarrel, so he pressed on.

'We will probably have passengers,' he said, 'and time is very much of the essence. We must make Rhapsody in the least possible time. Luckily, there is no other ship on Attalus capable of making the trip.'

'There's a fast yacht out on the tarpol,' Johnny interrupted.

'No good,' I said. 'Rhapsody's in the hyoplasm of a blue giant. There's not much distortion there, but the radiation and the gravity prevent p-shifters from operating. Only ramrods can reach the surface-lock.'

'Surface-lock?'

Charlot took over again. 'Rhapsody has only an internal

atmosphere. Its towns are built in several subterranean labyrinths. There is nothing on the surface at all. It would be as easy to live on Mercury.' Johnny was Earthborn, so he understood the allusion.

'As Grainger says,' continued Charlot, 'only ramrods are equipped to make landfall on Rhapsody. The solar hyoplasm has no effect upon the mass-relaxation drive, and they carry enough shielding to withstand the radiation. But ramrods are very slow, and there's only one within twenty light-years of her.'

'Where?' I interposed, already having a sneaking suspicion.

'By now,' he said, 'it's probably on Rhapsody. That's why time is of the essence. The ramrod probably took several days to make a landfall, but it had a considerable start. We must make the trip in a matter of hours.'

'Can we?' asked Nick.

'Easy,' I told him. 'No distortion, no trouble. These close-orbit worlds always look difficult, but there's no real trouble involved. Bright light and a big pull aren't going to bother the *Swan.*'

'We shall have no difficulty getting there,' said Charlot, in a tone which suggested that he didn't expect much difficulty once we were there, either.

'What are we going there *for*?' I asked tiredly.

He settled himself in his chair, preparatory to delivering a lengthy discourse. I sighed. The answer was obviously going to be buried in a lecture. If, that is, he bothered with the answer at all.

'God's Nine Splinters,' he said, 'were colonised by a religious sect known as the Church of the Exclusive Reward. Their faith is fundamentally anti-Monadist, and during the Monadist resurgence some two centuries ago, they decided that the only way to their own unique salvation was via isolation from the morally polluted galaxy. Their faith stresses the necessity of hardship and struggle for existence, if the Exclusive Reward which they seek is to be attained. Hence they chose for their colonies the nine worlds which were associated with two unstable and unfriendly suns. Not one of those worlds is really fit for human habitation. And they're about as isolated from the rest of the galaxy as it is possible to be without going out beyond the rim. The nine worlds are Ecstasy, Modesty, Rhapsody, Felicity, Fidelity, Sanctity, Harmony, Serenity and Vitality.

'The worlds are isolated, even from each other. They have no more than half a dozen ships of their own, and indulge in only so much intercommunication as is necessary to the continued existence of the colonies. Only Serenity and Vitality can really be said to be self-supporting, but most of the others are nearly so, and the bulk of the traffic is triangular, between Sanctity, Ecstasy and Harmony. The precise balance of supply and demand within the Splinter Culture is quite irrelevant, and so are the sordid details of their particular dogmas. What is relevant is that rumours have reached me that the people of Rhapsody have discovered something on their world which I might want. It is no use whatsoever to Rhapsody, or to any of its neighbours. It is potentially capable of making the world—or certain people on the world—very rich, so my informant claims, but the world doesn't know whether or not it wants to be rich. And the dogmas of the religion, of course, specifically forbid any of its adherents to *be* rich. All of which is causing a certain conflict between various members of the Church Hierarchy and their individual and collective greed.'

'What have they found?' asked Nick.

'I don't know,' he replied, sounding somewhat annoyed at the redundant interruption.

'What *could* they have found?' Nick followed up.

'It's difficult to say. Rhapsody, of course, exists by mining and by the conversion of heat energy into electrical power. The people are fed by organic conversion, but their efficiency is obviously limited. They have to be supplied occasionally with raw organics from the middle worlds of the system—that's Vitality and Felicity. The mining, if undertaken properly, might be an economical proposition, but of course the people have no interest in interstellar commerce. They supply only their own needs. I assume that whatever has been found has been found in the mines. I maintain an open mind as to its possible nature. Speculation is quite useless.'

'It sounds like a wild goose chase to me,' I said.

'Perhaps,' he conceded. 'But New Alexandria has chased a good many wild geese in its time, and the few that we have caught have amply rewarded us for our trouble. It is precisely because we have always been willing to try what no one else thought to be worthwhile that we are now the most influential world in the galaxy. Knowledge which is worthless in small quantities becomes immensely valuable in complete form. None of our time has ever been truly wasted.'

"That is a matter of opinion,' I said.

There were a thousand things he could have cited in order to support his argument. So many, in fact, that he didn't even bother. He just ignored me.

'Where does Mavra come in?' asked Eve.

'The political situation in the Splinters as a whole, and Rhapsody in particular, is in a state of perpetual confusion and flux. Today's exiles are tomorrow's heroes. Small heresies may so easily become divine revelations. In matters of belief, fashion is a powerful driving force. No religion is ever static, and when a faith is confronted with a problem like the one which has arisen on Rhapsody, viewpoints are subject to many forces which tend to move them about and spin them around. It seems to me that by taking Rhapsody's exiles back home at this time, I may be able to inject several friends into important positions within the Church Hierarchy. This may be valuable.'

'You expect competition, then?' I asked. 'This ramrod that you mentioned?'

'The ramrod belongs to an organisation known as the Star Cross Combine. By no means as large or as influential as the Caradoc Company, who were so unfortunate and so trouble-some in the matter of the *Lost Star*, but rich and ambitious nevertheless. I hardly think they will have taken precipitate action because of a rumour, but they might well have directed the captain of the ramrod to invest a few weeks or so in investigation. They might not, of course, and he might not be able to get there in time, even if they did. But that remains to be seen. A few hours invested in making friends can hardly do us any harm, whether Star Cross is involved or not'

'Suppose somebody else has become interested in the rumour?' asked Johnny.

'They'll be too late,' Charlot predicted confidently. 'Rumours reach New Alexandria very quickly. Star Cross's advantage was purely positional. And in any case, no one else is likely to go so far out of their way hunting—as Grainger so aptly put it—wild geese.'

He fell silent, and looked at us expectantly. There were no more questions. We seemed to be finished, for now.

It seemed to be a moderately easy way to pass the time. A great deal easier than hunting up the *Lost Star*, anyhow. Law or no Law, what could possibly happen to me on Rhapsody? Not that it was my kind of world, of course. I have an irrational distaste for the faithful, no matter which particular breed they belong to. Naturally enough, the feeling tends to be mutual. Even the most easygoing of people tend to find me mildly offensive—to begin with, at least.

I was suspicious of Charlot's story, but not enough to worry me. I assumed as a matter of course that the old man knew more than he was telling us. But if I was to be tied to him for two years, I was rarely going to find circumstances where I could be one hundred percent sure of what was on his mind. The New Alexandrian mind is basically twisted, and Charlot had a few extra twists over and above the call of duty.

All in all, I was pleasantly surprised that this operation seemed to offer little opportunity for disaster.

'When do you want to lift?' I asked him.

'As soon as possible,' he replied. 'You can attend to your various needs while I talk to the people from Rhapsody. It will take them some time to collect together their belongings, but I think we should be ready to go by midnight.'

'It couldn't possibly wait till morning, I suppose?'

'Midnight,' he stated definitely.

'We'll be ready,' promised Captain delArco.

The party broke up. Charlot exited at a fast walk. His hurry was showing. I guess he had a lot of sweet-talking to do. The Rhapsody crowd wouldn't make friends easily. Not even in response to the carrot of a free ride home. But I had no doubt that Charlot could talk his way into their good books, given an hour or two in which to do it. By midnight, Rion Mavra would be his bosom buddy.

'Not much of a job,' commented Johnny, as we headed for hot water and soap. He seemed quite down in the mouth about the dullness of it all. Apparently the harrowing trip through the Halcyon Drift hadn't cured him of his thirst for deep space adventure. He had real courage all right, but no sense of proportion.

'It'll be a cakewalk,' I said unenthusiastically. 'Relax and enjoy it. There's plenty of time yet to go shooting monsters on alien worlds.' That, I supposed, would be his idea of a good time. There's no accounting for taste.

At that time, I didn't exactly visualise my taking an active part in the happenings on Rhapsody. I certainly didn't see myself wandering around in the planet's black depths, alone, shattered, frozen and pursued. I suppose it was Johnny's sense of melodrama which involved me in the first place, but once I was loose, it was all my own work.

And all my own fault.

CHAPTER THREE

I should have been dead tired, but I couldn't go to sleep. It wasn't simply a matter of not daring to go to sleep, even if I was sitting on a highway. I purely and simply couldn't sleep.

After a while, I began to find the darkness oppressive. I once lived, for a while, on a world which was not unlike Rhapsody. The main difference was that it could be reached, even by p-shifters, because it was that much farther away from its primary. (Even so, it was never easy sliding the old *Fire-Eater* in and along an eclipsed groove.) But the culture could hardly have been more dissimilar. The air was always hot and loaded with odours. The background smell of sweat and the conversion machines was always masked by heavy perfume. Here, on Rhapsody, there was nothing like that. Not that the air smelled bad—this was a much bigger warren, and there were fewer people here—but where there were odours, in the towns and the mine workings, they were politely ignored, as if they did not exist. And it was a matter of politeness—the odours were never so perpetual that they could be blotted out of one's consciousness.

And on that other world, light was a treasure of immense value. The aesthetic existence of the culture was built around the qualities and uses of light. The people thrived on light—soft light, kind light, warming light, soothing light, sad light, angry light, jealous light, callous light. The rarity of light within the caverns enabled the people to find all kinds of beauty in the mere presence of it that other cultures, saturated by abundant solar radiation, could not hope to discover.

Again, nothing of that sort here. The inhabitants of Rhapsody were apparently content with their darkness. If anything, they had come to abhor light in any quantity. Their capital had been illuminated only by dim lanterns, placed haphazardly rather than in the locations where they would be most useful.

The Rhapsody people had eyes, and used them; there was no doubt about that. But they seemed to be ashamed of their eyesight, and they apparently rejoiced in the hardship of doing without it whenever it was convenient, and often when it was not.

One could, perhaps, imagine that the warrens here might develop an alternative aesthetic life from that of the other world. One might imagine their coming to appreciate the qualities of darkness, rather than of light, finding beauty and inspiration in shadow and obscurity. But that had not happened either. These people seemed to have no art and no concept of beauty.

Even their language had been modified only by loss. They had abandoned all the words describing the quality of light: effulgence, brilliance, sheen, iridescence, radiance, lambent, pellucid, lustrous, rutilant, luminiferous, incandescent, coruscate. Likewise, they found no use for terms describing bodies of light; not merely sun, but also nimbus, corona, aurora, spectrum, beam, halo, *ignis fatuus* and spangle. They did not trouble to differentiate between a glitter and a gleam, a glow and a glare. They were ignorant of the whole appreciation of brightness in all its forms. They lived by muted yellow lamplight, existing in an environment of dismal gloom. As though they were born and lived and died in veils or blindfolds.

And the corresponding enrichment of their language, which should have adapted their speech to their environment, was simply not there. They knew darkness, and obscurity, and murkiness, and shadow. And that was all. Nothing new to allow them to be in closer harmony with their world. The entire culture seemed to me to be somewhat subhuman.

Time to move, said the whisper, jerking me from my train of thought.

I permitted myself a slight groan as I got to my feet. My arms and legs seemed to have seized up completely in belated protest against the long crawl through the narrow fissure by which I had come to this spot. I flexed my fingers and kicked my feet. My hands were torn and the wounds were filthy. They seemed to have no feeling in them at all while I held them still, but as I curled the fingers they burned with pain. The little finger of my right hand caught on my belt as I tried to clean some of the dirt from the palm by rubbing it on my equally filthy shirt. The flashlight which I'd lodged there fell from its precarious position, and clattered on the stone floor.

Frenziedly, I dropped to my knees and began searching the floor with my injured hands. I found it, and flicked the switch anxiously. The light came on, and for a few moments it seemed abundantly strong. But as my eyes adjusted, I realised that it was very weak indeed, and could not possibly last more than a couple of hours.

It's not all that vital, the wind assured me.

'I'm not used to stumbling around in Stygian darkness. I come from a *normal* world, where people use their eyes.'

I've lived without sight before now, he told me. It's only a matter of using the other senses at your disposal. You have enough of them. With a little help from me, you can get by.

'I'll drive my own body, thank you very much,' I said. 'There'll be no more takeovers.'

Your insistence on my maintaining a wholly passive role in this partnership is quite ridiculous. I can use your body more efficiently than you can. It makes no sense at all to be so determined that you and you alone should exercise control of it.

'It makes sense to me,' I assured him. 'And you can't gain control if I don't want you to, can you?'

No.

Actually, I had my doubts about that. I wasn't sure exactly how far I could trust what the wind said about the limitation of his abilities. After all, he had never once mentioned the fact that he *could* assume control over my body until the occasion had actually arisen, at which point he had simply gone and done it.

I moved off, walking briskly along the passage. I considered turning off the flash and making my way by feel, which would have been moderately easy. But I didn't like the idea at all.

'I hope we're going the right way,' I said pensively. 'I don't really want to end up back in the capital with all those angry miners.'

Don't you know?

'Do you?'

It didn't occur to me to keep track, he said darkly. You're driving, so I assumed you knew what you were doing.

'I hope I do,' I said serenely. 'My sense of direction hasn't let me down before. Not often, anyhow.'

Not, of course, that I'd ever been called upon to navigate in a place like this before. In total darkness, with no sky but only solid rock, orientating oneself could hardly be easy. However, I reflected, the tunnel only went two ways. If I had completely lost my sense of direction, there was still a fifty-fifty chance that I was going the right way.

The passage curved right, and was joined by another coming from the left. I tested the air currents in both corridors. The new one had more or less still air. It swirled around near the entrance, because of the current in the main corridor, but it had no real current of its own. I concluded that it served merely to connect two tunnels which were part of the circuit, and therefore had no part in the circulation itself.

I followed the airstream around the bend, and on into the darkness. I could have taken the connector and gone through it to the other tunnel, which might have been arterial, and therefore warm. But there didn't seem a lot of point in searching out a warm tunnel when my real objective was habitation. Creature comforts could be attended to once I'd re-established contact with the human race—preferably some fraction of it which wasn't after my blood.

Switch off, directed the wind suddenly.

I complied, and saw the reason for the directive almost

immediately. In front of me, but a long way off, there was a faint glimmer of light. I glanced behind me, but there was only limitless darkness in that direction.

The light ahead seemed to be extremely feeble, but I knew that it would only be a dim electric bulb and it was probably not as far away as it looked. I hesitated, not over whether to go on or not, but over the matter of the flashlight. If I continued with it on, then I would be just as visible to an observer near the other light-source as that light was to me. It seemed sensible to keep my approach as close a secret as was possible, and therefore I eventually continued in darkness. I moved cautiously, and with a certain amount of trepidation.

When I reached the light, I found that it was a bit of an anti-climax. It was just a light, hanging from the ceiling. There was another some twenty or thirty yards on, and more after that. I presumed that I was coming close to a town. The abrupt termination of the 'street-lights' appeared to have no obvious ratio-nale except that the supply of cable had given out. It seemed a little pointless to light a small fraction of a road, especially when the job was done so inefficiently, but it seemed typical of the way things were done on Rhapsody.

From my point of view, though, the transition from dark-ness into light was an important one. Quite apart from allowing me to conserve the power in my flashlight, it had a noticeable psychological effect. I no longer felt like a skulker pretending to be a shadow, no longer a worm in Rhapsody's dirt, or a rat in Rhapsody's walls. I could see, and I could be seen, and there were no two ways about it. If I went on, then I walked openly, as a man among men.

A particularly disreputable man, by all appearances. In the tentative glow of the yellow bulb, I could see at last how bad I looked. My clothes, from neck to toe, were completely begrimed. They were not simply black, but slick and greasy by virtue of the amount of native protoplasm which I had encoun-tered. My face, I supposed, would be equally filthy. Certainly no one I might encounter was going to take me for an innocent citizen out for a healthy stroll, nor even a worker covered with the dirt of honest toil. It was patently obvious that I had been crawling through places where honest toilers were not wont to crawl.

But I hadn't really any choice. I stuck the flashlight firmly in my belt, and set off regardless, striding confidently and trying to appear perfectly self-possessed. But the road was still absolutely deserted. The dust beneath my feet wasn't the dust of centuries, by any means, but it was obvious that people didn't tramp back and forth along the corridor every day. Apparently the principle of isolation which was an integral part of the faith of Exclusive Reward applied all down the line. Perhaps the people in the town that I was approaching didn't even know yet about the state of affairs in the capital. If that was so, they probably wouldn't be nearly so disposed to clapping me in irons or shooting me dead the moment they saw me.

That was the nicest thought I'd had in ages.

On the other hand, what I'd seen of Rhapsody's children didn't lead me into thinking I might be welcome. Human or otherwise, most people are willing to *talk* to people who help them. But even Charlot had had a hard time getting through to Mavra's associates. Mavra himself had been forthcoming enough, but he was some kind of politician anyway. Anyone I was liable to meet in the caves would presumably be more like Mavra's hangers-on—Coria and Khemis. And I didn't much like what I'd seen of *them*.

CHAPTER FOUR

It was foggy.

It was always foggy on Attalus.

We had returned to the *Hooded Swan* with all due haste, arriving with a few minutes in hand of midnight. But there wasn't the slightest sign of Charlot or our precious guests. While we were attending to necessity and using a few rare hours of freedom to unbend our ship-clouded minds, Charlot had apparently taken it into his head to change the schedule.

'Damn him!' I said.

'He'll be along,' said delArco. 'It's probably taking them longer than he figured to pack their bags.'

'They can't own much,' I muttered. 'They came away from the Splinters in a spaceship.'

'We could go back to the port and have a drink,' said Johnny.

'At midnight?' I said scornfully. 'This isn't civilisation, you know.'

'Well,' said Nick, 'at least we know that Titus Charlot and his crowd can't be merrily socialising.'

'More probably cleaning out the local bank,' I said humourlessly.

The prospect of a long wait was most unattractive. The crew of any spaceship might be as happy as skylarks zooming their pride and joy between the star-worlds, but when the ship is on *terra firma* they need time to savour real gravity and real air, and time to imbibe a ration of dirtside living. A starman is a creature of two worlds: out there and down here. Each has its mode of existence. Upship personnel tend to develop agora-philia on a hop, and it takes a certain amount of downstairs routine to work it off. To be rushed around at breakneck speed and then left to hang about in the fog on the edge of the tarpol was nobody's idea of a joke.

By one o'clock (local) I was distinctly annoyed. I hadn't had any proper sleep for three days. The drug-induced ship cycle just isn't the same, somehow.

'Where do you suppose they've gone to?' asked Eve.

'We must have been over all the possibilities at least three times during the last hour,' I snarled. 'Give it a rest. Talk about the weather, or something. On second thoughts, make it "or something". I don't like the weather, either.'

'The port officer's not there,' supplied Nick. 'There's no light in the reception building. That's against regulations.'

'So report him,' I suggested. 'Hell, there are only two ships down, and *we* don't need a baby-sitter.'

'We've had one every other landfall we've made,' he pointed out.

'This is Attalus,' I reminded him. 'There aren't any police here because there aren't any criminals. There's nothing for the criminals to live off. Besides which, nobody knows we're here. The last job was a publicity stunt, remember? It wasn't us the crowds were interested in, it was the *Lost Star*.'

'We needed that police protection, though,' he said pensively.

'Nobody's going to try to assassinate me here,' I assured him. 'And you had nothing to worry about even on Hallsthammer. No one has anything against you.'

The boredom, of course, was solely responsible for the morbid vein of conversation. None of us really thought that anything untoward had happened to Charlot, or was about to happen to us.

'He's coming,' said Johnny suddenly.

'About time,' I said. 'How many maniacs has he got with him?'

'Can't tell. Fog.'

Charlot and his companions went directly to the ship, and we set out to join them. We met halfway across the tarpol.

'Sorry,' said Charlot briefly. 'They all wanted to go home, but they weren't sure that they ought to. It's been a long, hard argument'

He really did look somewhat fatigued. The peculiarities of the faithful had apparently been getting on his nerves somewhat.

There were seven people with him.

At first glance, they didn't look very much out of the ordinary. There wasn't a smile in sight, but it *was* the middle of an alien night. We didn't look happy either.

We loaded up without exchanging any pleasantries. In the interests of getting off the ground without further hanging about, even I gave them a hand with the baggage. There wasn't much as I'd predicted.

As we crammed them into the cabins, Titus Charlot identified them by name. I listened, and even learned how to tell them apart, though I wasn't particularly interested.

Rion Mavra himself was in no way distinguished. He was of medium height and complexion, with drab features. He looked to me like the perfect picture of a civil servant, although Charlot had described him as a politician. Judging by appearances, I decided that in all probability he was a failed diplomat without a future. At that time, however, I had no idea what kind of qualities it took to be a top man in the Splinters, or what shortcomings one could get away with.

Cyolus Capra, I remembered, was some sort of blood relative to the boss. He looked more alive than Mavra—insofar as any of them could have been said to look alive. I charitably put it down to the hour and the situation, but it later transpired that the corpse-like expressions were their natural attributes.

Cyclide, Mavra's wife, was a small, compact woman who had obviously seen better days and wasn't trying too hard to convince herself or anybody else that they were still around. She didn't look pushy enough to be the power behind her husband, or interested enough to have kept pace with him. The Church of the Exclusive Reward apparently had old-fashioned ideas about the place of women in society. Cyclide always seemed to be half a pace behind her husband.

The two other men, Pavel Coria, and something Khemis—whose first name I forget—looked counterfeit. By which I mean that they gave the appearance of being reasonable imitations of humankind without quite having the feel of the real thing. They reminded me vaguely of the way Lapthorn used to speak about the 'faceless hordes' that populated the worlds of the core. 'Human vermin' was another expression which he might have used. And Lapthorn, unlike me, was quite an admirer of his own species. I took an instant dislike to these two, and they never did the slightest thing which might tempt me to dispel it as an overly harsh first impression formed under unfortunate circumstances.

The remaining two females did not seem to be attached to Coria and/or Khemis, and neither did they lay claim to any relationship with the Mavra family. One of them was called Camilla, and was very young and very plain. Her existence seemed quite irrelevant, save that she occupied a certain amount of space.

Angelina, on the other hand, was just young enough, and far from plain. She was the only one of the seven who clearly showed symptoms of having been born and bred in a warren. Her skin was dead-white, and had an odd, lustrous quality which made it look silvery when illuminated obliquely. Her hair was very pale blonde, and also had a noticeable sheen. Her eyes were pale grey, and her lips bloodless. In addition, she had a fragility of frame and feature which made her ghostliness seem very appropriate and even beautiful. Very few people are actually suited to the appearance of etiolation, but Angelina was one of them. I found Angelina most definitely attractive.

It didn't strike me as particularly odd that Angelina was the only one whose aspect betrayed her origin. The cave-dwellers with whom I'd been associated in the past had all sported magnificent suntans and hair all colours of the rainbow. All courtesy of lamps, skin salves and bottled pigment, of course. It did occur to me, as I looked at Angelina, that Rhapsody didn't have the sort of culture which would go overboard on cosmetics—and, in fact, was extremely unlikely to be able to come by supplies of cosmetics. But Mavra and his friends had presumably been on-surface for some time, now, and would have been forced to adopt a fake suntan simply for protective purposes. They had presumably dyed their hair muddy brown in order to avoid standing out among the populace of their host planet.

Once I was in the cradle, preparing for the lift, I eliminated all thought of our human cargo and its place of origin from my consciousness. But the wear and tear of the previous trip, coupled with the highly unsatisfactory Attalus landfall, had left its calling card. I was unusually slow, and I could feel an edginess about my nervous state which was most definitely out of the ordinary. For the first time since I took control of the *Swan* I missed a transfer. I had a grossly inexperienced engineer underneath me, of course, but I really don't think it would have made any difference if it had been Rothgar. Johnny did nothing wrong—it was me who made the mistake. I was surprised, and extremely annoyed. I was, when all was said and done, the self-confessed best pilot in the known galaxy. (As good as I could be, at any rate.)

I caught the second transfer—just—and got the bird into a groove with a minimum of manoeuvring, but I could still feel my temper fraying. I'd been building up a current of resentment ever since the lift from New Alexandria, but it was that missed transfer which really set the edge on me. After all, I'd lately piloted a ship in and out of the heart of the Halcyon Drift at tremendous speed, without a mishap, and I couldn't be blamed for yielding a little to the legend of my own infallibility. It may seem strange that such a small thing could upset me so much, but I honestly think that if there was one single incident which could have sparked off the whole chain of events which followed in the caves of Rhapsody, then that was it. A fractional slip by mind and hand, and maybe three or four minutes lost forever.

We were well under way, and going very fast indeed—forty thou or more—when I finally abandoned her wholly to the groove and sank back into the cradle. I lifted the hood from my eyes, but didn't push it all the way back.

'ETA?' asked Nick.

'Three hours and a few minutes,' I told him. I couldn't be bothered giving him the standardised time. By standard it might be mid-afternoon, but as far as I was concerned it was still one o'clock in the morning plus thirty or forty standard minutes. Like most spacemen, I didn't use a wristwatch. If you keep standard time, it doesn't tell you anything, and if you keep local time you have to adjust the watch every time you make a drop. Lapthorn had carried one, and laboriously altered its time and setting every landfall, but I could never be bothered, Besides, Lapthorn had always been around so that I could ask him.

Eve came into the control room with Charlot. 'All settled now,' she said. Neither she nor Charlot made any mention of the poor take-off. That didn't make me feel any better about it. A sarcastic comment would at least have allowed me to expend a little vitriol in a reply.

'They're a peculiar crowd,' said Nick idly.

'You can't expect them to act like tourists,' said Charlot. 'They're exiles. They don't know what sort of a welcome or lack of it they're going back to. They've only my word. I think only Mavra believes there's anything actually to be gained. And the white girl, perhaps.'

'Do the rest of the people on Rhapsody look like her?' asked Eve.

I interrupted with a brusque laugh. 'Hardly,' I said. 'Just as pale but as ugly as sin.'

I didn't look around, but I could imagine the sharp glance which Eve would have thrown in my direction.

'They'll be pale,' said Charlot. 'What else would you expect? Some members of the Church hierarchy might be able to get cosmetics, but I can't really think that they'd take much trouble over them. The Order of the Exclusive Reward is somewhat ascetic. Self-decoration would undoubtedly be frowned upon.'

Which didn't really add much to what I'd said.

'Are they all members of the priesthood?' Nick wanted to know.

'They're all members of the priestly *caste*,' replied Charlot. 'None of them is actually ordained. But I don't believe the Church maintains a great many ordained ministers. The whole caste seems to bear a collective responsibility for the maintenance and dissemination of the dogma, but the actual part played by any one of them might be any of half a dozen things. Political, philosophical, clerical, or simply advisory.'

'In other words,' I put in, 'the Churchmen are a hereditary aristocracy who maintain their privilege by saying that God meant it to be that way. They have all the plum jobs and give all the orders.'

'True enough,' said Charlot. 'I'm not trying to make these people out to be any better than they are, so there's no need to be derisory. You're not scoring off me. I only want to deal with these people—to buy whatever they have to sell with whatever they want in return. I'm as critical of this type of faith as you are, but it's not going to advance my cause if I say so in your kind of terms. I'd be obliged if you would limit your insults and your mockery once we're landed, as well.'

'I'll say what I like,' I said.

'No doubt. But I'd appreciate it nevertheless if you didn't go out of your way to be unpleasant. And I'd be even more grateful if you could bring yourself to exercise a little self-restraint.'

The content of the words was sarcastic, but the tone in which they were delivered was not. Charlot was occasionally very difficult to fathom.

In the course of the trip Mavra and two of his companions—Capra and Khemis—appeared in the control room for a look around. If it had been up to me, I'd have locked them out, and I think Captain delArco was of the same mind. But Charlot was sparing no possible effort to make friends. They didn't ask questions and they didn't look impressed. They prowled around for a while, with the same hangdog expressions on their faces that they'd worn during embarkation. Eve spoke to them, and so did Charlot, but their attempts at communication met with blank-wall indifference. Capra answered, but flatly. Khemis merely grunted. Mavra made an effort, but it was obvious that he was keeping his opinions and his goodwill under strict guard. I didn't envy Charlot having to trade with such people.

Eve, who had most contact with the ones who stayed below all the time, later complained of their aloofness and unreasoning distaste for her efforts. I reminded her that these were a people who had made a faith out of collective and individual alienation. They were effectively disbarred from being nice people, and also from appreciating the efforts of nice people on their behalf.

They were, in short, quite unlikable.

Only an hour passed before I had to put the hood back on and negotiate us into the system. This was, the time-consuming element of the trip. The deep space was of no concern at all, but the blue giant warranted a lot of respect, and I had to approach tentatively while I located Rhapsody, plotted an approach which gave me the best chance to avoid trouble on account of the radiation levels, and began a slow approach.

I didn't make any more mistakes.

Not aboard the *Hooded Swan*, anyhow.

CHAPTER FIVE

'Well now,' I said to myself, and to the wind, 'there are two kinds of people who might be useful. Ones who know what's going on and can tell me. And ones who don't know what's going on and therefore couldn't possibly have anything against me.'

The whisper agreed.

'I think for the moment I'll be content with the latter.'

He agreed with that as well.

I was standing in black shadow, looking out into the dull-lit street. The town was built in a gigantic cavern—even in places like Rhapsody, people prefer to make their homes in the wide-open spaces. Because of the woeful inadequacy of the lighting, I couldn't gauge the size of the cave or guess how many houses there might be. But the ones I could see were laid out in blocks about ten or eleven dwellings long. The fact that they had used a block layout suggested that the town was a good size. It seemed reasonable to assume that it would serve as a dormitory area for the miners, would also contain such social and economic units as coexisted with the miners, and would also have its fair share of Churchmen/aristocrats. Presumably the elite would live in the good parts of town, and even by the standards of Rhapsody that wasn't where I was standing now. It wasn't simply that the streets were dim, or the houses small and grubby. It was the atmosphere of poverty. The aristocrats might not be well-endowed by galactic standards, but the reality of poverty is always relative. There was no mistaking that this was the wrong side of the non-existent tracks.

A few people had passed by while I hid in my alley and watched. They hadn't glanced sideways, or even looked up. They'd merely ambled on about their business, hiding their eyes from the faint light which helped them on their way. I didn't know enough about local habits to judge whether it was local 'night' or the middle of the rush hour.

I'd had ideas about passing for a native, but even a casual glance at one of the locals assured me that it simply wasn't possible. Apart from their maggoty whiteness, they were all thin and moved in a peculiar stooping shuffle which obviously required long practice to perfect. I was too dark, too big and I walked like a surface-dweller.

I stuck out like a black spider in a termite nest.

Even with clean clothes on, I would only be a somewhat less hairy spider. And if I were to acquire clean clothes they would have to come out of a cupboard or off a body. Nobody here hung out the washing to dry in the sun. I didn't really fancy mugging some poor innocent and stripping him, and it certainly wouldn't endear me to the local populace if the indiscretion were discovered. It seemed preferable to adopt the ancient but not very honourable profession of sneak thievery.

In my long and arduous career as a trader and general bum, I have often had cause to appropriate articles to which I did not have clear legal title. But I have never regarded myself as a talented or accomplished thief, and I have never made a very serious study of the science of removing other people's property without attracting their attention.

Ergo, I was in some doubt as to how to go about the task of changing my clothes. And I was therefore doing what I always did when I was in doubt.

Hesitating.

You'll get caught, prophesied the whisper gloomily.

'It's a possibility,' I conceded. 'But what has to be done has to be did.'

He was considerate enough not to remind me that even if I

succeeded, I'd accomplish nothing but the opportunity to hesitate further while I faced more and more difficult problems. He probably would have, had I not been already bearing it in mind.

I waited until the street was clear, then oozed out of my protective alleyway into the main thoroughfare, and sidled up to the nearest door.

It was locked.

I kept going, trying each door in turn, determined that the first one that opened would define my target for me.

I think it was the sixth door which actually yielded to my touch, and opened noiselessly. I slipped quietly inside, and eased the door shut behind me. It closed with the faintest of clicks, and I congratulated the lightness of my touch.

The slender hallway was dark and silent except for a weak line of light which was visible in the crack under a door that was directly in front of me, some three metres away.

I reached out with my foot to search for the stairway that I knew must be there. I guessed that it would be on the right-hand side of the hallway, and I was right. I took the flashlight from my belt, and flicked it on momentarily just to be sure that I had the layout correctly deduced. Everything looked quite ordinary. A house is a house, on Penaflor or in the warrens of Rhapsody. I didn't leave the flash on while I went upstairs, not because I was afraid that it might attract attention but because I was desperately afraid for the future of the charge it held. A hundred times I had vowed to myself that I would never again step out into alien territory without belting a full charge into the thing.

The stairs were made of stone (naturally) and didn't creak. I took great care not to shuffle my feet, and to test the height of each step individually. So far as I could detect, I was as quiet as the proverbial mouse. Unfortunately, I had forgotten that people who live in perpetual near-darkness, liberally spiced with absolute pitch-blackness, tend to develop an unusually acute sense of hearing. Burglars must have a very difficult time on Rhapsody. Amateur though I was, the ease with which I was detected suggests that there must be easier ways to make a living.

The door with the sliver of light beneath it suddenly opened wide, and a woman came out. She brought no light with her, and she was stepping from an illuminated room into darkness. But she saw me immediately.

The light that was behind her made her snow-white hair gleam. Her hand rested on the side of the door, pale and skeletal, like the hand of a corpse. Her face was shadowed, but somehow I could sense the deathly whiteness of that, too. It was as if that door had been opened by someone six weeks dead.

I didn't wait to find out whether she was going to scream— I shot back down the stairs and out into the street. It was flat panic—reflex action. Sure, I knew what the people of Rhapsody looked like—neither the gang I'd ferried back nor the miners who'd grabbed us after we landed had scared me or nauseated me in the least. But this was different—I was a fugitive in a world of darkness, lost in a labyrinth of cold stone. This was alien territory—*truly* alien, for all that it was a world of men. I just hadn't been ready for that door to be opened by something which didn't look human. I hadn't adjusted. Maybe I should have stopped to think, and come out with some prize comment like: 'Hello, I'm a burglar.' But my reactions didn't give me time to stop and think.

The street was still empty. I ran back the way I had come, heading for the entrance to the tunnel, some vague idea forming in my mind about re-thinking the whole operation. But I never got there. I paused at the corner of a small alley, looking out towards the slash of shadow that marked the way out. I could hear footsteps behind me, moving fast but not running. I could also hear voices—but they were coming from the tunnel. The way out was blocked.

I had only one clear way to go—out of the alley, but away from the tunnel mouth—and I wasted no time. I tried to run quietly, but on the stone pavements it was impossible to stop my footfalls making a fair amount of noise. There was no shout to indicate that I had been seen, but I knew that if the alarm was given, and people began to search, it would only be a matter of minutes before I was found. I had to hide. But the houses had no back yards, no garages. There seemed to be no small niche into which I could dive with a respectable chance of waiting until the fuss died down and silence reigned supreme once more.

I rounded a corner and cannoned into someone who was trying to round it the other way. We both stumbled but I managed to regain my feet almost immediately. The man I'd collided with was bowled right over—he was younger and much lighter than I. He came to rest in a pool of light cast by one of the street-lanterns. There were at least three other people on the street, and they all looked my way. I knew that I was both clearly visible and obviously an intruder. I ran across the street, aiming for the darkest alley in sight. No one ran towards me, there was no shouting. I crossed two more streets into two more alleys, and then I paused. The moment the echoes of my own footsteps died, silence fell. I didn't believe that I could have shaken them off, but they weren't running after me.

I was confused.

What now, hey? said the wind, with just a trace of sarcasm.

'Okay,' I muttered, '*you* suggest something.'

Let's go home, he said.

'Home to where?' I wanted to know.

Home to jail, he said. We were safe there. It's not our concern.

'I don't *like* being in jail,' I told him. 'It's not civilised.'

We can't run away for ever, he pointed out. We've got to make contact with *somebody*.

There was a door beside me. I couldn't see it, but I could feel it. I groped for a moment or two, and then my hand settled on the handle. Almost automatically, I turned it. The door gave way. It was just as dark inside as out. I slipped inside, and closed the door behind me, very quietly.

I stood for a moment in absolute darkness, and then I flicked on the flashlight. I was in a short, narrow corridor. There were doors to either side, and one door at the far end, about twenty feet in front of me. I tiptoed down the corridor, straining my ears to catch the faintest sound. I could hear something beyond the end door, and when I pressed my ear to the plastic I could make out the sound of a voice. I switched off the flash and carefully eased the handle of the door, pulling it open just a fraction of an inch.

I looked out into a large—by Rhapsody standards—room with a high arched ceiling. The only illumination came from a series of small flickering flames set in a row against the back wall. In front of the flames, with his back to them, was a man in jet black robes and a tiny black cap. He was talking in a low drone, obviously reciting something he knew by heart. I knew that he just had to be a priest.

He hadn't much of a congregation—it must have been an offpeak service. There were less than a dozen of them, all kneeling on a bare stone floor, with their heads tilted forward so that they almost—but not quite—touched their foreheads to the floor. It looked very uncomfortable.

The wind didn't bother to ask, What now? He knew I was already wondering. I knew that in the old movies when the hero hides in the church the priest never gives him away. But the movie-makers never heard of the Church of the Exclusive Reward, and the priesthood of Rhapsody had sure as hell never seen a movie.

I was just about to go back and investigate the other doors when one of them opened. Silently, I heaped a few curses on my luck, which seemed determined to get me caught. Someone came out into the corridor. He didn't bring a light. I couldn't see him and he couldn't see me, but he knew I was there.

'Who is it?' he asked. His voice was thin and sharp.

I switched on the flash, and directed the weak beam at his eyes. He looked like a vulture, with a bald head and à big hooked nose. He was dressed in the same black robes and cap as the man conducting the service. I saw his white face for just an instant before he protected his eyes with his loose sleeve.

'You can't bring that in here,' he said harshly. 'Where did you get it?'

'It's mine,' I said.

'You're an outwolder,' he said, moving his head sideways to try and get a glimpse of me behind the glare of the flash. 'You've no business here. How did you get here?'

'I just came to see the sights,' I said drily.

'Get out of here,' he said. 'Get out and don't come back. Go back to the capital and get off this world. You're not supposed to come here.'

He obviously didn't know that I'd broken jail. Maybe he didn't even know there was a panic on. Clearly information didn't travel very fast around here. I let the beam of the flash fall away from his face, so that he could uncover his eyes.

'I need some clean clothes,' I said. 'And some food. And a wash.'

'Your money's no good here,' he said. 'We won't give you anything. We don't want anything to do with you. Just get out and go away.'

I shook my head slightly. No alarm. No threats. Just: go away. He simply didn't want me near him, didn't want me in his church. It occurred to me that it was quite possible no one had chased me at all. No one had been in the least interested in me. Nobody knew who I was or why I was here. Nobody even wanted to guess. They just wanted me to go.

On impulse, I thrust the door behind me wide open, letting it hit the wall with quite a loud bang. I stepped out into the main body of the Church and stood there, waiting for them to look at me and react.

The priest stopped droning, and he looked at me. I couldn't make out the expression on his face. The others just stayed exactly as they were, heads bowed, apparently totally oblivious. I shone the flashlight at them, but they looked neither towards the light nor away. They remained completely still, as if they were carved from the stone on which they knelt.

I wanted to say something—something loud and offensive, to see if they'd react to that. But I couldn't think of anything to say. I shone the beam at the priest.

'Well?' I said.

The other priest stepped past me, hugging the wall as if he wanted to stay as far away from me as possible. It might have been because I was so dirty, but I didn't think so.

'He was in the corridor,' explained the man who'd found me. 'I told him to go away. He's an outworlder.'

As this revelation was made—quite unnecessarily, as it was obvious to anyone who cared to look—I flicked the light back to the worshippers, hoping that it might awaken their curiosity.

One face—only one—turned my way. It was a small boy, and he took just one quick glance at me before he looked away again. I saw an expression of utmost horror in his pale pink eyes.

The priests weren't scared of me, I knew that. If anything, they felt revulsion. My mind went back to the faces of Rion Mavra, of Coria and Khemis, and the beautiful Angelina. And the gunmen. I could see now what had been behind their stony expressions and their silence. Perhaps—in Mavra's case, at least—a long way behind, deeply buried beneath diplomacy and necessity, but there nevertheless. How else could a chosen people regard those who had elected to go to hell?

'You must go,' said the priest whose service I had interrupted. 'You cannot stay here. Go, at once.'

'Where?' I asked him. 'Where do I go?'

'Anywhere,' said the priest. 'There is nothing for you here. The people will not see you. There is nothing for you here. You must go.'

'I want something to eat,' I said. 'Some clean clothes.'

'No one will give you anything,' he said.

'Suppose I take it?' I said, feeling an edge of real hatred creeping into my voice.

'We will not see you,' said the priest, and promptly looked straight ahead again. He took up his recitation again. I glanced back at the priest who had discovered me. He was studiously looking elsewhere, and while I stared at him he assumed the air of one going about his proper business and moved away, quietly and respectfully.

Deliberately, I shone the beam into the eyes of the speaking priest. He did not blink. I moved closer, making the beam more intense and more direct. It must have hurt him, but he did not show by the slightest sign that anything was happening. Suddenly, I had become the invisible man.

I went back into the corridor, and began opening the other doors, searching for food and water and clothing. I found water, and I found a thick overall which enabled me to replace my filthy trousers.

I washed my hands slowly and carefully, realising for the first time that they were badly blistered. I am inordinately sensitive about my hands—a pilot has to have good hands to handle a ship well—and the blisters brought home the fact that I had plunged neck-deep into bad trouble. I paused to wonder what was wrong with me, sure that I would never have acted this way in the old days. But that soon passed, and I began to wonder once again what I was going to do next. The weird attitude of the people had caught me completely by surprise. What was the point of being free if nobody would see me? But I knew full well that if I tried to go back to the capital, steal a spacesuit and get back to the *Swan*, the armed miners would have no difficulty in seeing me and shoving me right back into my cosy cell. And this time they'd be more careful about letting me out.

When I was good and ready, I went back outside.

Okay, said the wind, so you're an ace burglar. You can steal what you like. So what?

'Somewhere,' I said, 'there has to be someone who can tell me where to find whatever it is that's caused all the trouble.'

Sure, he agreed. But how are you going to get him to look at you, let alone tell you what he knows?

I didn't know.

CHAPTER SIX

Once upon a time, long before the *Javelin* ploughed a ditch in the black rock of Lapthorn's Grave, Lapthorn and I had occasion to set the *Fire-Eater* down on a world which had pretensions to being a planet of beauty and elegance. The people there thought very highly of themselves and had a generally low opinion of everybody else. As a nut cult, I suppose, they were no less unusual than the worm-like citizens of Rhapsody, but they certainly seemed to have a lot more to be proud of (and conceited about). However, I don't like cults of any kind, and I probably wouldn't have liked them any better than I liked the Exclusive Rewardists even if they hadn't been so consistently nasty to me. They thought that Lapthorn and I were pretty poor specimens, both physically and idealistically, and they lost no opportunity to offer us evidence of our failings.

In the main square of the port where we made landfall stood a monument which carried a proud boast of their ambitions and their philosophy. The statue was corny enough—a stylised athlete in the classical mould. The ancient Greeks had produced hundreds just as good, but because the cultists had plonked theirs a thousand light-years from ancient Greece they had a much higher opinion of themselves. The inscription on the pedestal was the motto of the cult.

It read: MEN LIKE GODS

Lapthorn had studied the statue and the inscription with all due seriousness when we first landed, and I could tell that he was impressed. But he was of asthenic rather than athletic build, and never put on weight no matter how much he ate. It would take a lot more than healthy exercise and clean living to turn him into a reasonable imitation of a superman. This, mercifully, prevented him from becoming involved with the culture and philosophy of the world, and the way that the inhabitants went to great lengths to insult us soon drove out any least vestige of admiration which he might have harboured for them.

Hence, when temptation struck me, as it occasionally did, he was unable to muster sufficient disapproval to counsel caution. One night—the last of our intended stay—I, with Lapthorn as accessory before and after the fact, did wilfully and maliciously deface the sacred statue.

I inserted the word DON'T into the inscription.

I thought it was funny.

So did Lapthorn.

They threw us in jail for ninety days (local). Fortunately, the world turned on its axis faster than most.

Until I landed on Rhapsody, that was the only time I was ever in jail. It may seem peculiar that a career so long and checkered as my own should not have resulted in other periods of incarceration, but it was a fact. My innate cautiousness and honesty had conspired to keep me safe from the versatile arm of the Law of New Rome, and simple diplomacy had sufficed to keep me out of trouble on a purely local scale.

That single episode had instilled into me a healthy regard for the dangers of trespassing on other people's idiosyncrasies. It also added fuel to my strong dislike for those of definite and exclusive faith.

I actually remembered and rehearsed that incident as I approached Rhapsody, but I make no claim to a prophetic gift. I was as surprised as anyone else when we were jumped as soon as the drive-unit was cooled.

I had taken off the hood, and was relaxing in the cradle with my eyes shut. It hadn't been a difficult approach and landing at the speed I'd elected to adopt—as evidenced by the fact that I'd been able to reflect on old times—but there are proprieties to be observed. A space pilot should always look as if he's been through hell and a half to get where he is.

Charlot and Nick had gone down to attend to the passengers, and Eve was disconnecting my electrodes with one hand and preparing my shot with the other. We weren't in any hurry, and while we exchanged a few innocuous and irrelevant remarks some fifteen or twenty minutes crept by. I would have been moderately content, in fact, to stay on board for the duration. We need our *terra firma*, of course—as I've said—but we prefer it accompanied by air and sky and sunlight.

I heard the inner lock swing shut with an unusually loud thump. I presumed, of course, that somebody was getting out. But a few seconds later, an anonymous figure in a surface-suit scrambled into the cabin with an indecent amount of haste.

He was waving a gun.

At first I thought it was Johnny, because he was the only person I knew who habitually waved guns for no good reason. Then I realised that it wasn't one of our suits, and I knew we'd been jumped.

I couldn't see his face because of the black glass visor in his helmet, but I could imagine him watching me like a hawk. All-seeing and predatory.

He pointed the gun at me and said, 'Get out of the chair.'

Strangely enough, that order made me feel better. No spaceman would refer to the cradle as a 'chair'. Ergo, I conclusion jumped, he hadn't come to steal my ship. It was me he wanted.

I disentangled myself from the straps, and stood clear of the cradle.

'Right,' he said. 'Now, one at a time, get down the ladder. Put your suits on slowly.'

The others were already being shipped through the lock, two at a time. There was another heavy with a gun at the bottom of the ladder. They had already seized such of our armoury as was accessible without grubbing in the hold. Eve and I donned our suits with dramatic care. Remembering what conditions on the world were liable to be like, I took a flashlight and secured it inside the suit. The gunman didn't object.

I was the last to leave. One gunman went out with Eve, the other with me. There was a third waiting outside, and that was all. They had apparently been given no trouble at all. I was very grateful that Johnny hadn't been inspired by our numerical superiority to put up a fight. The *Hooded Swan* wasn't a big ship, as starships go, and with seven passengers, five crew and three gunmen aboard she was distinctly overcrowded. The consequences of a beam battle in a sardine can are dreadful to contemplate.

We were escorted across the surface of Rhapsody away from the *Swan*. They didn't leave anyone on board, and they permitted Nick to secure the lock against potential invaders.

I'd put us down in the twilight zone, at the required latitude, within a couple of hundred yards of the surface-lock which gave access to the principal warren. The pinpoint accuracy was a great compliment to my piloting, but no one expressed gratitude that we didn't have far to walk. The surface was all dust-drifts and rock-jags, and wasn't suitable for strolling in the evening, but we had no difficulty in obeying the instructions which our captors sent over the open call circuit. They marched us in Indian file to the vast lock, which gave us access to the capital. I looked around briefly, and caught sight of one other ship—presumably the Star Cross ramrod—a couple of miles away towards daylight.

We were permitted to desuit in the reception area under the lock. I was allowed to retain the flashlight, but not to remove any of the other potentially useful things that were secreted in the suit, under the guise of standard equipment. (Like, for instance, food concentrates and the emergency bleep.)

We were now privileged to clap eyes on our captors for the first time, while they crammed us into a hand-operated hoist.

The heavy mob looks the same the universe over. They have never really escaped the influence of the clichés laid down by the earliest exponents of the art of strong-arming. They always have big shoulders and slack features, and a casual swing to their movements deliberately styled to suggest that they can— and maybe do—bend iron bars between their fingers. Our welcoming committee was trying hard—if subconsciously—to give this overall impression, but they weren't very good at it. Gangsters may be born or made, but these men had had gangsterism thrust upon them. They looked as if they'd rather be pecking away at a rock face, and that was probably their normal occupation.

'What the hell goes on?' asked Nick, while the hoist descended noisily. It was Charlot's picnic, of course, but Charlot hadn't bothered to protest or demand to be taken to their leader, so perhaps Nick thought it was up to him to expel some hot air. Mavra and company seemed to take the whole affair very fatalistically.

'Shut up,' said one of the gunmen bravely.

'There's no need to add insult to injury,' I remarked.

'Shut up,' he said again. He obviously didn't feel up to explaining the situation. A man of action.

'As a matter of simple curiosity,' said Charlot oilily, 'are you institutionalised or freelance?'

No answer.

I rephrased the question for them. 'He means, are you the regular cops or did you just take up the habit?'

Still no answer. It's possible that they still didn't understand the allusion, but I concluded that it was more likely they weren't going, to say anything more. I admire a man who can take his own advice.

We didn't get to see much of the local scenery. They hustled us out of the hoist into a dark corridor, and promptly split us into three groups going three different ways. The men of Mavra's party were one group, the women of Mavra's party the second, and the crew of the *Hooded Swan* the third. They marched us up and down long corridors that were all grimly similar. This was the first time we encountered the full force of Rhapsody's sporadic lighting system. Some corridors had only one lamp, often not centrally placed. Others had two, and were well-endowed by the local standards. Not one of the bulbs was brighter than a wax candle.

Nick, Eve and Charlot were hustled through a door into a minuscule cell. Johnny and I were taken down the passage a little way and shoved into a similar one. It was just as small and just as crowded.

There was a man lying full-length on the bunk. He looked up at us with the ghost of a smile on his face. He was an offworlder, like us. I presumed that if there were other cells, they must all be full of outworlders. Either that or the cavemen were not in the least concerned about our comfort. The cell was about eight feet by six. The bunk was six by four and a toilet took up at least a sixth of the remaining floor space.

'Standing room only?' I remarked, gazing steadily at the man sprawled on the bunk.

He got the hint, but he didn't move.

'Nice to see you,' he said, probably with a certain amount of sincerity. It couldn't have been much fun on his own. 'Where did you blow in from?'

'Attalus,' said Johnny, giving nothing away.

'You company men?' he asked.

'No,' I said.

There was a pause.

'Maybe I'd better introduce myself,' he said. 'I'm Matthew Sampson. I....'

'You drive a ramrod for the Star Cross Company,' I told him, to show that I knew what was what, and in the fond hope that he might be persuaded to tell us something we didn't already know. 'You the captain?'

'That's right,' he said.

'I thought so. Nobody but a starship captain would take up all the bunk room while we stand.'

He must have taken a dislike to my attitude, because he didn't move his big feet.

'Who the hell are you?' he asked, instead. His voice was still level and friendly, as if he were trying hard not to take offence.

'My name's Johnny Socoro,' supplied Johnny.

'I'm Grainger,' I added.

'The guy who reached the *Lost Star*,' he said, with sudden apparent enthusiasm. 'Say, you did us a big favour there. Caradoc hasn't got its face back on straight yet. It lost four ramrods in the Drift, did you hear?'

'I was there,' I told him. I didn't bother to tell him that I'd actually seen the ramrods blow. I didn't feel like explaining how it had happened.

'So you're from New Alexandria,' he said pensively. 'You got that crazy ship here—the *Hooded Sun*?'

'*Swan*,' I said coldly.

'It's here, then,' he repeated.

'It's here.'

'And you're after the payload?'

'Payload?' I asked with sarcastic innocence.

'Come on, man,' he protested. 'We're all in the same jail. There's none of us going to be treasure hunting while the war's on. We might as well sit down and talk about this thing like civilised people.'

'How civilised?' I wanted to know.

'Look, man,' he said. 'There's no point in either of us being dog-in-the-manger when neither of us has the loot. I mean, why not be friends? When it comes to the crunch and the locals want to make a deal, you hold the cards, remember? You got New Alexandria behind you. I only got a boss who'll hang pictures with my guts if I don't do things his way. And your ship has ten times the pace of mine, if it comes to a race. I'm no fool, friend, and neither are you. We can make a deal here and have the whole thing settled by the time they let us out.'

'You're sure they're going to let us out?'

'Ah, the guys with the guns are only trying to tidy things up and keep all the wheeling and dealing on top of the table. It isn't a revolution, you know.'

'It might be by now,' I said, remembering that we'd just

thrown Rion Mavra back into the political maelstrom.

'No,' he assured me. 'That's not the way they do things around here. It'll all be settled soon, after a lot of talky-talky. The only change from our point of view is that we'll be dealing with the whole kit and caboodle instead of just Jad Gimli or any other Sons of the Whitewashed Skeleton operating under their own banner. Say, nobody else is here, are they? It is just you and me?'

'As far as I know,' I told him, 'there are no other parties involved. Nor are there likely to be.'

'That's good,' he said, relieved. 'Now, how about some honest talk? Spirit of good, healthy competition. Open season on the cavies, huh?' He sat up on the bunk. 'Take a seat,' he invited cordially. I sat down, after carefully brushing the place where I intended to sit with the edge of my hand. Sampson gave me a pain. He was about as genuine as a Nineteenth Century antique spaceship.

'If, as you say, we have all the advantages, why on Rhapsody should we work out a split with you?' I asked gently.

'Ah!' he said. 'But do you know what the payoff actually consists of?'

'No,' I said, 'and neither do you or you wouldn't be sitting there making a fool of yourself talking a load of utter garbage.'

'It was worth a try,' he said, trying to laugh it off.

'No, it wasn't,' I said. 'The whole line was a bad joke. You're also way off beam. I'm not the head man in our outfit. Captain delArco outranks me, and if that isn't enough, we've got the New Alexandrian owner along as well. You haven't got a cat's chance of getting anything out of this shebang.'

'Thanks a lot,' he said drily. 'They really will have my guts, you know.'

'Think yourself lucky,' I told him. 'I remember four company captains who got themselves killed.'

'Big man, eh?' he said sourly. 'Tangle with Grainger and you lose your pants?'

'It's not me, son,' I told him, deliberately patronising. 'It's you. This crash bang, fast buck space opera stuff isn't going to get you anywhere but in trouble. What do the companies do to you guys? I know that everything happens in a flat rush these days, and everybody wants to rule the galaxy, but I just don't see how giving starships to whizz-kids like you is going to make anybody a fortune. The turnover in ships and men must be horrifying.'

'We aren't running the rim for half a loaf and a hunk of cheese,' he said, 'I know how you made your reputation, and any tramp out of New York port could have done the same. But things don't work that way now we can get ships into the sky at any rate we choose. What matters now is pace and guts. That's what makes fortunes.'

'Pace you've got,' I said. 'I'll grant you that.'

He got angry, but he cooled himself almost immediately.

'OK,' he said. 'OK. There's no point in sitting here arguing. You don't think much of me, and we both know that I haven't much chance of swinging this deal my way. Whatever the bloody deal is. But can we at least talk sense?'

'What kind of sense?' I asked quietly.

'You're not the boss. You just fly the ship. Great. How much do you want to cut me in?' He swung his eyes to where Johnny squatted on the floor. 'That goes for you, too.'

Johnny just looked at me. He knew full well how much I hated Charlot. He also thought enough of the Grainger legend to fall in with whatever I decided. He expected me to agree, because of the twenty thousand which would buy my contract with Charlot.

And I was very tempted.

But also cautious.

'That's very kind of you,' I said. 'But I don't see that either of us is in a position to make deals.'

'I told you. They'll let us out'

'So what? That doesn't automatically give either of us a bite at whatever cherry they're hiding down in the caves. We've nothing to deal with. Either of us.'

'My company will back me'

'You don't know that! How can you possibly know, when we don't have the slightest idea what these people have for sale?'

'You can at least let me know whether you're interested.'

'Not until I know what's going on. Once I find out what all this hassle is about, I'll be in a position to estimate what can, will and ought to be done with it. Until then, nothing.'

'I'll tell you what I know,' he said. 'The top man—they call him the Hierarch—is called Akim Krist. He doesn't talk money, just dogma, by all accounts. The man I tried to deal with was Jad Gimli, who was first in on the find after the guy who originally leaked it. Krist found out what Gimli was doing, and began spreading poison all around the Church. The big men, who run a kind of Church council, split at least two ways, and everybody started howling heretic at each other. Somebody—maybe Krist—armed some of the miners and asked them to keep the peace. The miners shoved me in jail, for convenience, while the council got itself reorganised and began to talk strategy instead of hurling accusations. I guess they must have started by now, but it'll probably take them an age to get things sorted out. They aren't much concerned with practicalities, only with getting their damned consciences squared. I haven't seen Gimli since they shut me up, so I don't have up-to-date information. All I know is that they have to work out some kind of deal eventually, because the last thing they want is to keep the hot potato in their cellar for all time. All the talk will be about what kind of deal. I can't see them turning out New Alexandria for Star Cross on any kind of pretext, for all that Gimli's on my side—and anyone else he can bribe. Your side has the bigger money and the better line in holiness. The only way I can see for me to keep my job is to get the loaf sliced, and to grab some away from you. Sure, I'll be late getting it back, but when Star Cross finds I've got some of the goods it'll reckon I did all I could. Now, I don't care who I buy my slice from. I've offered an open contract to anyone who'd listen. You can include yourself if you want, or not, as the case may be. Fair enough?'

I considered the content of the diatribe carefully. 'Seems fair,' I said. 'I'll remember you, if the cards happen to fall that way. But don't take that as an offer. I'm making no deals until I see the gold at the rainbow's end. Which may be never while we're stuck in this place.'

Sometime during Sampson's speech, Johnny had developed a crick in his back from sitting folded up on the floor. He'd got to his feet and seemed to be occupying his time by staring morosely at the implacable door of our cage. He tested the bars that were set in the window—the sort of standard gesture one associates with prisoners.

He looked back at the pair of us, with a wicked gleam in his eye.

'Like to bust out?' he asked.

'No,' I said. 'They have guns. They might shoot'

'How do you mean?' asked Sampson, who was understandably attracted by the idea.

'I can get us out,' said Johnny confidently.

'Sure,' I agreed. 'He balances himself on the doorway and when the guard brings in our food, he drops on the poor sucker like the avenging angel. It's all in the movies. I've seen it. Go ahead and try, heroes.'

'No,' persisted Johnny. 'It can be done.'

'You can pick the lock, I suppose,' I said.

'That's the point,' he mocked back. 'We don't have to pick the lock. This isn't a real jail cell. It's a punishment cell—for penitents to work off their sins. It wasn't designed to prevent a determined escape. It hasn't got a real lock. Only bolts on the outside. And there's enough space in the crack for us to work them back with a knife-blade or even a comb. It world only take a couple of minutes, if we took a bolt each.'

Sampson was off the bed like a shot, peering into the crevice between the door and the wall.

'He's right,' he said. 'A kid could break out in five minutes fiat. And I've been here the best part of twenty-four hours.'

'Hang on,' I said. 'There are still the miners out there, and they still have guns. What the hell are we going to do once we're out?'

'Whatever you want,' supplied Sampson. 'Maybe there's nothing we can do. But it's a chance to find out what goes on here, and it's better than rotting in here. If all you want is to get away, you can always head for the lock and space out.'

'You don't seem to get the point,' I pressed. 'There are guys out there with guns. With the exception of my trusty flashlight, we're completely unarmed.'

Sampson made a noise that was intended to indicate scorn. However, I wondered again, did guys like that get to run starships? Low cunning and brashness, I supposed.

'He's right,' said Johnny. 'Better be out there than in here. We can get clean away before they realise we're gone'

'Clean away to where?'

Common sense was on my side, of course. But Sampson thought he was on to a loser anyway, and desperate measures were needed to put him back into the hunt. He didn't have the slightest idea what might be done, but he was keen to try it. I could imagine him sending out missiles to plough up a contortive domain in a dark nebula, and blowing himself to bits for his trouble. This breed of spaceman couldn't last for long, inexhaustible supply of ships or not. Simple natural selection would consign them all to hell.

And there was no arguing with Johnny. He wouldn't learn to sit still until he was badly burned by playing with too much hot property. This was his idea, and nobody was going to talk him out of it.

'Let's get on with it,' he said, to Sampson. He pulled his penknife out of his pocket, and set to work on the upper bolt.

'Bugger you,' I said. 'Play at Count of Monte Cristo if you want to.'

So they did.

I never really believed in digging tunnels with belt buckles and guards who were carefully dispersed so as not to disturb any potential escape plans. But I had to admire the speed and facility with which those two managed to open that door. It was straight out of the comic books. It had real style. I was suitably impressed.

Sampson went off like a rabbit, but Johnny paused to say, 'Come on, you fool,' before he too disappeared.

Well, what could I do? My nerves were still ragged from the rigours of the last four days. I was sick of being manipulated by circumstance. I *needed* to act, to do *something*, whether it was constructive or pointless or just plain crazy. And I'd look a real fool when the miners came back and found that one of their pigeons had staunchly decided to play by the rules and not indulge in irresponsible chicanery.

I went.

I glanced at the bolts as I left, and remarked silently that it was a damn silly way to design a door.

CHAPTER SEVEN

There was the sound of running feet. The darkness and the echoes conspired to prevent me from defining the direction from which the sounds came. But they were close. There was no need for me to dive for the nearest cover. I'd been skulking in deep shadow whenever the opportunity presented itself.

There was a brief pause, while one set of footsteps died away, and then there was a gunshot. In the wake of the staccato echoes, many footsteps started up again. There were obviously several pursuers and several pursued. I crept forward to the nearest corner, intending to take a quick look at the lighted street in the hope of seeing something which might give me an idea what was going on. Then somebody stuck a gun barrel into the small of my back.

I froze, and a hand grabbed the collar of my borrowed overall.

'*Quietly*,' hissed a voice, and the gunman began to pull me backwards. He was fairly gentle, obviously because he wanted me to comply with his wishes and keep it silent.

He backed me up through twenty metres or more of total shadow. He then reversed our positions, and pushed me into the half-light which filtered around the corner from another street.

'He's an offworlder,' said an incredulous whisper. It wasn't the man who held me but an invisible companion. I had to admire the way they moved in absolute silence. I hadn't suspected the presence of either one until I was touched, although their initial approach might have been masked by the gunshot and the runners.

'Who the hell are you?' whispered a second voice—that of my captor.

'My name's Grainger,' I told him, in a hoarse whisper.

'What are you doing here?' he breathed.

'I escaped from the capital. They had me in prison.' I saw no logical alternative but to tell the truth. I could hardly claim to be a tourist.

'I think we're in the clear,' said the other voice, this time from the corner.

'Whose side are you on?' continued my interrogator.

'Nobody's,' I said. 'I'm just trying to find out what's going on.' He released my collar, but kept the gun barrel pressed against my spine.

'Give it ten minutes,' he said to the other man.

'What are you doing on Rhapsody?' This from the second man, who had moved back from the corner again. He was obviously used to moving about in pitch-blackness with the lightness of a ballet dancer. And whatever he was wearing on his feet, it wasn't boots like mine.

'I'm a pilot,' I explained. 'My owner heard that there was something up for sale here, and he came to try to buy it. We brought some exiles back with us.'

'Exiles?' he hissed. 'Coming *back*?'

'That's right,' I said, wondering why he'd reacted.

'Rion Mavra?'

'He was one of them.' Suddenly, I could hear him breathing. Something connected with Mavra or with exiles in general was obviously stirring him up.

'Who are you?' I asked.

'Outcasts,' he said briefly, as if that explained everything.

'It doesn't mean a thing,' said the first man, talking to his compatriot. 'Mavra coming back. You know that. We still don't exist.'

The pressure of the gun eased slightly, and I contemplated trying to grab it. But these men didn't have anything against me, and I wasn't in any overt danger of being shot, just so long as I did what they told me. I decided to let things ride.

Then they pushed me up to the corner again. After a moment's pause, we went out into the street. Here I was able to see them for the first time. One was tall and thin. He walked in front of me in a cat-footed version of the local gait. He looked big and awkward, but he moved confidently and silently. The other—the man behind me, who covered me with his gun—was short and cadaverous. He was older. Both men were as pale as albinos, but they wore black caps to conceal their hair and their faces were discoloured with dirt. Only their hands and eyelids betrayed the real whiteness of their skin.

'Come on,' said the short man. 'Move it. We can't hang around here.'

'We're all right,' the other assured him. 'The miners went after the others.'

'Why don't we just split, and leave this one behind?'

'No,' said the tall man. 'He might be able to tell us something.'

I should be so lucky.

We moved out of the township and into a corridor. It was lighted in the same perfunctory manner as the one by which I'd gained access to the town, but it didn't look like the same one. It was narrower and deeper.

'Look,' said the short man, to me. 'The lights give out along here. You put your hand out onto Tob's shoulder. He'll lead you. I'll be right behind you.'

'I've got a flashlight,' I said.

'Light! Forget it. You got to get used to the dark some time, kid. This might as well be it. Can't be afraid of the dark all your life.'

I was tempted to point out that people who did not live out their lives on Rhapsody could, in fact, afford that very luxury, but I refrained. I also refrained from fishing out the flashlight. I put my hand on Tob's shoulder, as I was instructed, and allowed him to lead me.

'The gun's still here,' the short man reminded me, once we

were again entombed by darkness. 'Don't think I'll be shooting blind, neither. I'll hit you if I have to.'

'Don't worry,' I assured him. 'At the moment I need a few friends far more than I need a couple more enemies. I'm on your side, at least for now.'

'Stop talking,' he said. 'Keep moving.'

We seemed to go around endless bends, as though we were negotiating a maze. But the tunnels which we used were always a comfortable size. There was no crawling or climbing. The general direction of our journey seemed to be downward, and we were usually heading into slow-moving warm airflow, down arterial passages toward the hotcore. At first, we moved with exaggerated caution, stopping occasionally while one or other of the men satisfied his doubts as to whether it was safe to continue. But as time went on they both relaxed. They didn't say much nothing relevant, anyhow. They were probably guarding their tongues on my account.

It seemed a long way, but it was all easy. Our destination turned out to be a big cave not unlike the one where the town had been built. But this one hadn't yet been appropriated by the property developers as a suburb full of desirable family residences. Such buildings as there were had been thrown together, by inexpert hands, and they sat in a miserable huddle surrounded by acres of empty space. It was obviously more than a temporary resting place, but it was certainly not civilisation even by the somewhat elementary standards which applied in the Splinters. The only thing which seemed out of the ordinary about the cave itself was the fact that it provided its own lighting. Its vast dome was sprinkled with patches of luminescent bioplasm. The light was not strong, but compared with the feeble lamps characteristic of Rhapsody it seemed to me to be as glorious as daylight. It occurred to me that the only reason why this cave had *not* been appropriated for colonisation could well be the presence of the abundant natural illumination.

The people who *had* moved in here were presumably the outcasts of Rhapsody's religious society—and so, in fact, the two who had grabbed me had termed themselves. Any society which maintains itself by rigid principles—whether they be laws or beliefs—inevitably has occasion to cast out or otherwise dispose of its misfits. The Splinter culture, being basically non-violent, would naturally choose expulsion. For the privileged, expulsion to Attalus. For the underprivileged, a simple get-lost-and-look-after-yourselves. Which couldn't be easy, on a planet which lived so close to the survival line.

There were half a dozen other men visible in the ramshackle village as we passed through its streets. If you can call the gaps in between stone tents 'streets'. The lanky man gently prised my fingers from his shoulder. I'd been so taken up with first impressions of the place that I'd omitted to realise there was no further need of being led.

He then ushered me into one of the largest of the dwellings—one which was more or less centrally placed. It was remarkable in that it was the first building in the warren I had seen which possessed windows. Inside, it was grim and grey, but it seemed more like a real house than the solid boxes of the town and the capital. It had only two rooms, but these were large and furnished adequately, if crudely. The bed was a strung frame like a spaceship bunk; the table was a cunningly balanced edifice of stone. The chairs were strung frames as well, and had apparently been improvised from various sources.

'Very nice,' I commented to Tob. 'Almost palatial, in fact. But a little more light would brighten it up considerably.'

'You can see, can't you?' he replied.

'After a fashion.' But he, of course, was used to nothing more. He had never seen a sun.

'Wait here for Bayon,' he said.

'Who's Bayon?' I asked.

'It's his house. He's the boss.'

'A priest?' I guessed.

He laughed. 'Ain't no Churchmen here. They get along without us, we get along without them. Now, you just sit. Bayon won't be long. And don't try to run away.'

'I'm quite well aware of the pointlessness of running away,' I told him. 'I'm on your side, remember?'

'Yeah,' he drawled sarcastically. 'I remember.'

Then he left; presumably to talk to his friends. I looked out of the window for a while, but nothing of any consequence seemed to be happening. So I went back and sat down.

I was very hungry. It was a considerable time since I'd last eaten, and that had only been gruel. Not that there was liable to be anything better available here. Normal worlds have fake food, and good worlds have real food. But Rhapsody only had converters. Probably obsolescent and inefficient converters at that. I tried to imagine anything more lifeless and unappealing than gruel. I found, somewhat to my surprise, that it was easy. Everyone complains about gruel, but everyone eats it. One could do a lot worse.

My thoughts of hunger were interrupted by the arrival of Bayon. He came in, escorted by Tob and two other men, obviously prepared for a session of interrogation. Their manner was not exactly hostile, but it was determined.

Bayon was a tall man, like Tob, but of thicker build. For a troglodyte, he was something of a giant. But his frame wasn't fully fleshed out. He could have put on a lot more weight without beginning to look fat. Life must be hard for the refugees. He carried a power rifle—the only one I'd seen in the possession of the outcasts. The other men carried less sophisticated weapons.

'Well,' I said, 'have you decided whether to eat me yourselves or feed me to the crocodiles?' The allusion was totally wasted.

'I'm Bayon Alpart,' said the leader—the man I'd already tagged as the big cheese.

'My name's Grainger,' I told him. 'I pilot starships. You, I take it, have no particular vocation except staying alive.'

'We're outcasts,' he said.

'I know'

'You'd better tell me what you're doing here,' he said. 'The whole story. Don't leave anything out.'

I sighed, and went over the whole sordid story again. I told it all straight, and I didn't leave anything out. I suspected that these were people I could work with, people whose interests might be persuaded to coincide with my own. I saw my first real chance of getting the whole mess sorted out, and actually doing something with the pieces.

It was a longer story than I'd anticipated, and it took a long time. My audience seemed totally engrossed and adequately entertained.

I even managed to forget, for a while, that I was on the brink of starvation.

CHAPTER EIGHT

'It might well have been a mistake to skip jail,' I said. 'I was safe there for the duration. But curiosity drove me out. I wanted to get into the action.

'I went the other way—the way that Johnny and Sampson didn't go, that is. They headed back the way we'd been brought in. I didn't see much point in going that way, so I didn't. I think Johnny might have paused to release Nick and the others, but I can't be certain. Once I'd decided to run, I ran, before the alarm could be given and we were beset by hordes of trigger-happy miners. I was seen and chased, naturally enough, since I was in the capital. But most of the people I passed either didn't care or caught on too slowly to the fact that I was escaping custody. They had fifty chances to grab me, and missed every one. Nobody shot at me, presumably because flying bullets and beams would have endangered the citizenry.

'I spent an age wandering around in the tunnels, completely lost. Then I found the town, appropriated a change of clothes, and stepped outside again. At which point I was seized by your compatriots, who were engaged at that particular moment in evading pursuit by someone else. And that's the whole story. I was dragged into this blind and I still don't know everybody's Big Secret. Once I've found out what that is all about, I might try to work out some way of making a profit to compensate me for all my trouble. At this particular moment I feel troubled enough to contemplate any and all offers up to and including blackmail.'

'You want to come with us?' asked Bayon suspiciously.

'That depends entirely on what you want to do.'

'Can you get us offworld?' he said bluntly.

'I don't know. I've got a ship, of course. Not exactly my ship, but I've already explained that. I'm perfectly willing to lift you off, if there aren't too many of you, but it would depend on Charlot. And, of course, on if and when the miners and the council decide to let us have our ship back.'

'This man Sampson—he could also transport us?'

'Subject to the same condition, yes he could.'

'And if we could provide him with what he wants, he would do so?'

'He'd be falling over himself. But the miners hold control of his ship as well as ours, remember. And the council seems more likely to deal with Charlot. New Alexandria has a lot more to offer.'

Bayon thought about it for a few minutes. His point of view seemed pretty clear. If he could get his hands on the goods—or part of the goods—he could make his own deal with Sampson while the council was dealing with Charlot. As an idea, it looked to have merit, but as a scheme it had a lot of problems. We hadn't got the goods, we didn't know how to contact Sampson, and Sampson couldn't get his ship offplanet unless the local gentry let him. More or less the same objections stood in the way of our trying to set up a separate deal with Charlot.

'I don't know whether I can trust you,' he said.

'I can only offer you my word,' I replied. 'I'll promise to do my level best to get you off Rhapsody, if that's what you want.'

'Will you act as our spokesman?'

'Sure, if that's what you want. But what do you intend to do? Do you know what this fabulous treasure is, or where it is?'

'I know where,' he said, 'but I don't know why.'

Somebody in the group which accompanied Bayon muttered something. I didn't catch what he said, but I gathered that he wasn't in favour of Bayon telling me what he knew.

'Get out,' said Bayon, over his shoulder. 'All of you. There's no need for you all to stay. You've heard what he has to tell.'

'You think there's a real chance you can get us out of here?' said Tob.

'If the council is willing to let us go back to our ships, and lets you come with us, I can certainly carry you to Attalus. Provided that my owner agrees. Even if he doesn't, Sampson would probably carry you.'

'Out,' said Bayon, waving his hand to dismiss Tob and the others.

'Wait a minute,' I said, feeling that I was now on an adequate footing to ask favours. 'Before we go any further, have you got any food? I haven't eaten in days.'

'Get him some soup, Tob,' said Bayon.

'Soup?' I queried.

'Watered-down muck from the converters,' he said. 'We have to steal it, usually. Anyone in the towns caught supplying us is liable to be sent to join us. A very Exclusive Reward for helping their old friends. But it's easy to steal. The Churchmen ignore us totally, and everyone else is supposed to do the same. The men at the converters get blamed if anything is missing from the supply, but at the same time they're not supposed to recognise our existence in order to stop us taking the stuff. They compromise to various extents, and we generally don't find it difficult to come by enough to keep us alive.'

Tob reappeared, with a bowl full of semi-dissolved gruel. It was only lukewarm, but it was something which I could use to fill the hole in my stomach, aid I spooned it down rapidly.

In the meantime, Bayon told me what he knew.

'They found a sealed cave,' he said. 'Broke into it by accident while they were hacking away at the rockface down in the mines. They were petrified at first in case it was another warren, and the interconnection was going to play all hell with the airflow. But they were lucky—this time—and it was only a chamber. Part of this warren, I think, but probably waterlocked. The grotto was full of shiny stuff, like this cave. There was no fuss at all for two weeks or more. Then, all of a sudden, every member of the council was accusing every other member of all kinds of crimes. I don't know the details, because we get the news late down here, and it's always vague. But there's something in that cave worth a great deal off this world.

'We tried to get into the cave, today, to get a look, but we were too late. Two weeks ago we could have walked in and everybody who was around would have been looking the other way. Today, there were men with guns at the grotto who decided to relieve the boredom by shooting up a little air. The air they chose just happened to be occupied by us non-existent persons. I don't know how they'd have got around the problem of disposing of non-existent bodies, but they weren't playing games. They chased us up to the town, and we split up there. It was easy to lose them once we were out of the tunnel.'

'You didn't get to see inside the cave, I suppose?'

'No. I don't know what's in there. But it probably wouldn't be obvious anyway. They didn't find it for some time.'

'They weren't looking for it.'

'Even so, it can't be very big.'

'What do you think it could be?'

He spread his arms wide in a gesture of frustration. 'How could I know? You're the spaceman. You travel from world to world. You know what's valuable, and what kind of thing is most likely to come from worlds like this one. You tell me.'

But I couldn't.

After I'd finished the soup, I realised that it was a long time since I'd had any sleep, as well. I was surprised to find that I wasn't very tired, despite the fact that I'd been on the go for a long time, but the idea of sleep was nevertheless a very attractive one.

'You know,' said Bayon, 'whatever it is, it's a great big joke on all of us. Our ancestors cut themselves out of the star-worlds hundreds of years ago. There's no trade. The Churchmen make every effort to ignore the stars, just as they make every effort to ignore us. They don't want to know about the *real* human race. And then up comes a find which could make any one of them, or all of them, very, very rich. All those years of living in utter poverty in conditions far more conducive to misery than to piety. All that holiness stored up as credit for the eternal reward which is to come. And now this. Money by the ton. Our whole life is founded upon the assumption that we are not and never could be wealthy. And suddenly, we are. What are they going to do? Can they really deny the existence of this as well? Can they really stare a fortune in the face and ignore it?'

'You live here,' I said. 'You tell me.'

'They have to come to terms with it,' he said. 'There's no other rational course. Our ancestors may have had the best of reasons for quitting galactic society. The fact that they hated it would be reason enough, wherever the hate came from. But we no longer have that hatred. We can't hate the galactic civilisation because we know nothing about it. We have the doctrinal legacy of our forefathers, but not the emotions which shaped it. We live by a creed that is no longer supported by need or desire. But it is all we have to live by. If it were to be abandoned—even if it were seriously questioned, life on Rhapsody would become intolerable. Any violation of the creed has to be punished by exclusion from the exclusive society—excommunication, supposedly total. My group has sixteen outcasts. There must be similar groups in the other warrens. There must be other groups on every world in the Splinters. If women were expelled as well as men we'd have equal shares in the planet in time. The population of the towns has been declining for a long time. There are fewer of us now than there were when the entire Church decamped from the starworlds. The whole organisation is a guaranteed loser. There are only two roads out of these caves. One leads back to the stars and the other goes straight down to hell. Extinction isn't a very Exclusive Reward.'

'They didn't tell you all that in the local schools,' I said. 'Do you get so much time for contemplating the unfairness of your situation?'

'We're not so primitive as all that,' he said. 'We live close to utter squalor, but we're not ignorant. We have our teachers and our scientists. The Churchmen and the miners are the pillars of the community, of course—the top and the bottom. But no society exists just like that, as you must know. There's always filling in the sandwich. We came *out* of galactic civilisation, remember. Our ancestors were there. They knew what it was about, and they took from it what they cared to call clean. That included education and thought. They didn't ask that their beliefs should hold up on blind obedience alone. They prepared the jargon and the arguments. They had answers to the questions; they didn't simply duck them. We're descended from an advanced culture, Grainger—we went *back* into the caves. We aren't a direct relic of the old troglodytes, and you'd be a fool to think we are.'

'You think the Churchmen can cope with the problem, then?' I said. 'You reckon they'll survive without schisms, witch-hunts and revolutions?'

'They'll survive,' he assured me. 'There's a lot of life in the old dogma yet. They could keep it stuck together for a hundred more years yet. It will beat them eventually, but they'll fight to the end. While Krist and the hard core of truly devout believers can use the accusation of heresy against anyone who disagrees, they retain the only power which there is on this world. Life here isn't easy on any terms, but at least the faith gives you a reason for existing. Once you're an outcast and condemned to unbelief, you're nothing. There's nothing to make it all bearable. More than three-quarters of those excommunicated over the last three years have committed suicide within a matter of days. Even the rest of us have difficulty in keeping some kind of hope alive. Getting off the planet is only part of that hope. We have to hope that we can find some kind of life out there with the evil stars. It doesn't feed *my* hope to know that Rion Mavra came back instead of disappearing into the galaxy for good. Some of the others think it means something, but they don't know what. They greet anything new which happens with determined optimism. It's what keeps them alive.'

'They didn't exactly treat me like the best thing to happen to them since the day they were born.'

'They're afraid of you. They're afraid to trust you. You're promising them the moon, remember, with an offhand expression which implies that to you it doesn't matter a damn whether we stay here till we rot or fly away with you. It's not a matter of little consequence to them—it's life or death—a second bite at the cherry of Exclusive Reward, a new impossible dream. If they'd been able to handle the realities of their situation they'd likely have killed themselves with the rest. These are the ones who can survive on self-made myths.'

'And what about you? You seem to know so much, to have all the answers at your fingertips. Where do you fit in?'

'Me?' he replied. 'I'm as incurable optimist. I'm too clever to be realistic. I can always invent a bright side to go with every dark thought. I'm the only man in the warren whose mind isn't clothed in black.'

I'm no born optimist myself, but I had to admit that the idea of a planet of fatalists wasn't very pretty. There was more darkness on Rhapsody than could be explained by the environmental restraints. I was going to be very glad to get back into daylight again. There might well be insane elements in galactic society, but there was nothing to touch Rhapsody.

'So what do you think we ought to do?' I asked, returning to the point at last.

'For a start, we can take the grotto.'

'By firepower?'

'It shouldn't be necessary to kill anybody. We know these caves a lot better than the good citizens. We can get there without any trouble. The guards will see reason when they compare the numbers.'

'And then? Do you think you can shoot your way to the lock and carry the booty away into space aboard the pirate vessel *Hooded Swan*?'

'No,' he said. 'But I think we can make a deal. I think we can make some arrangement which will assure us a ride out of here. Once we have the price of our passage, there'll be no stopping us.'

'Unless they seal you in and blast you out. Believe me, Bayon, a display of force usually breeds big trouble. Fire always gets fought with fire.'

'Not in the Splinters. Our culture is founded on talk, not on violence. We can do it, and we will do it. You'll help us, because you're committed. You take orders from me, now.'

I wasn't really surprised by the sudden hardness and hostility in his tone. It was perfectly clear that Bayon saw me only as a means to his particular end. He wanted to use me any way he thought he could. Like his followers, he could never bring himself to trust me enough to do things my way. He thought he knew best and he was going to push things the way he thought they ought to go. There would be no arguing with him.

I had to go along. He was probably more dangerous than the miners and the Church, so far as my state of health was concerned.

And besides, if I was on anybody's side, it would have to be his. Believe it or not, I sympathised. I wouldn't condemn anybody to live out their life in this filthy pit if they didn't want to.

And on top of all that, this was my best chance of cutting myself into the profits. On Rhapsody, where the Law of New Rome was non-existent, possession might well represent all ten points at issue when it came to deciding who owned what.

CHAPTER NINE

So now we know, said the whisper.

'Like hell we do. What kind of a fortune could possibly be buried in a cave on Rhapsody? It doesn't make sense.'

It has to make sense, he pointed out. Charlot is here. Sampson is here. They may not know what it is, but it has to be real—make no mistake about that. The problem is that you can't see the sense.

'Can you?'

You're in a better position to guess than I am. You've been on worlds of this type before.

'And you have access to all my memories of those worlds. But there's never been a world quite like this one. The people on those other worlds lived and acted like people. This is different. It's possible the idiots only think they've found something, and are raising hell over nothing at all.'

You shouldn't allow your dislike of these people to lead you into underestimating them. They would love to believe that there is nothing in that grotto of theirs. If they do believe it, it's because they can't refuse. As your new ally has pointed out, they are not ignorant except by conscious effort of will, which applies only to certain areas. They have their analysts and their logicians. Somebody knows what is in that cave and has checked their guess very carefully indeed. It doesn't matter who did it—only that it could be done, here no less than anywhere else. The fact that they have refused the galaxy's values does not make them blind to its prices.

'Well, you know what kind of thing brings a price these days as well as I do. Knowledge. Saleable ability. Alien science and alien technology. But there's none of that in the caves of Rhapsody.'

I think you'll find that the tremendous success of New Alexandria hasn't been simply in the collection of data. The New Alexandrians—including Charlot—are, in their own right, great scientists. The original purpose of the Library, don't forget, wasn't to provide leverage for galactic power, it was to provide for the needs of the pure research workers of the star-worlds.

'I know all that.'

That's hardly surprising, since I'm picking it all out of your brain. But it needs calling to your attention, because it has a bearing on the current problem.

'I don't see how.'

The New Alexandrians owe all their wealth not to alien knowledge but to their own ability to use and develop what they have found there. Their principal role is not collecting but adapting.

'In other words,' I said, 'you reckon it's something new. Not vulgar cash convertibles like radioactives or gemstones, but something peculiar which has properties no one's ever come across before.'

That's about the size of it. No amount of mineral wealth could possibly command the kind of respect that this find does. They could simply sell that to Sampson far a new set of conversion machines, and carry on exactly as before. This is more important than that—probably important with respect to the ethical considerations of the Church, as well. There seems to be more trouble here than would be warranted by a simple question of whether to involve outsiders or by private profiteering.

'You could well be right there,' I conceded. 'The Church of the Exclusive Reward does seem to be getting itself unduly steamed up. Improvised police forces don't spring up overnight unless extreme matters of internal politics are involved. And Charlot must have known about the political angle, or he wouldn't have taken the trouble to provide himself with a local politician *en route*. They didn't throw Mavra in stir with us, despite the fact that he was officially an exile. His past political sins appear to have become unimportant in the light of the current conflict.'

We don't actually know that Mavra has been welcomed back into the fold.

'They certainly weren't ignoring him, like they were supposed to.'

Not at all. You're confusing Mavra with Bayon. Bayon has been excommunicated from the faith. Mavra was merely expelled for political reasons. He still qualifies as one of the faithful.

'Maybe. But that's by the way. The question we've just set up is what the mystery *thing* might be able to do. If its properties are what make it so valuable, it must be able to do something we can't do already.'

Cheap power. A perpetual motion machine.

'Let's not be ridiculous. You don't dig up perpetual motion machines in caves. Are you trying to be funny?'

Of course not. Nor did I mean to imply that there was a perpetual motion machine in the grotto. Merely that something in the cave is capable of evolving power in an undiscovered fashion, which might ultimately lead to the development of a perpetual motion machine. I thought that was quite obvious and straightforward.

'Well, it wasn't. And it's ridiculous. Let's at least think of examples which don't blatantly contradict the laws of physics.'

I contradict your precious laws of physics, he pointed out.

'Yeah,' I remarked, without enthusiasm. 'Well, maybe they found another one of you.'

Without a host, he said, scornfully, I'd be hardly likely to wind up in a place like this. And even with a host I'd have difficulty getting into a sealed cave.

'You were free-living on Lapthorn's Grave.'

Dormant, between hosts. I didn't start off like that, you know. I was born into a mind.

'No,' I said, 'I didn't know. You may have access. to my memories, but I don't have access to yours.'

I can give you access, he said, with a sudden eagerness which made me very wary indeed.

'No !' I said, with some vehemence.

It wouldn't be difficult, he said. I can imprint them in your mind. It'll take time, but think what it could offer you. I was once...

'*I don't want to know*!' It was virtually a mental shriek. I didn't want to know. Not anything. Not ever. I wanted no part of him.

My abilities saved your life and your ship in the Halcyon Drift, he said.

'So you did me a favour,' I retorted. 'Well, I didn't ask, and even if I ought to be grateful, I'm not. Let's just say that once paid for your keep. You've rented space in my mind and you've added some time to my life. So okay, we're all square. But we aren't lovers, and we never will be. Just leave me alone. Don't do me any *more* favours. Right?' I was on edge, and I was pretty tired. Perhaps I let my temper loose and said more than I should have. But the thought of what he might be able to do with my mind and my identity just got on my nerves. I was scared of him.

What about the guessing game? he said, a trifle bitterly. Have we finished?

'There's no point,' I said. 'Making silly suggestions about perpetual motion machines or super-ray guns or planet-eating bug-eyed monsters is only going to give me bad dreams.'

You've had enough of talking to yourself for one day, he said—and this time there was no mistaking the bitterness.

'I was talking to you,' I said. 'Now I want to stop talking to you and sleep, if that's okay. It's been a hard day.'

You don't talk to me, he said. You talk to yourself. All you want from me is an echo. Well, you can't hide from me, Grainger. I'm here and you have to learn to live with me. You can't pretend you're crazy—you're not the type. You have to acknowledge me. You don't live in a black cave, you can't simply choose not to see me. Even if I can't harm you, Grainger, I'm *here*. Remember that.

Then there was a funny sensation in my mind, just one fleeting instant of it, like a lead weight falling on top of me... and through me...

Then I cut out.

CHAPTER TEN

I woke up to soft, silvery light filtering through the window-slit.

It seemed only normal and natural in the first few seconds, until I remembered that I was in the caverns of Rhapsody, and then—for a moment or two—what was normal became horribly abnormal. Almost immediately, of course, I made the connection between the light and the luminescent organisms of Bayon's village. But that single moment of fear caused by the slowness of my reactions after waking up was strangely disturbing, as though I were adapting myself to the black reality of Rhapsody. That was something I didn't want to do. I wanted to remain separate—a part of an entirely different world. To a large extent, what we are depends on what we perceive, and I had no wish for my senses to be rebalanced to accommodate the whims of Rhapsody's culture.

There are three senses associated with what we call sight: dark/light perception, depth perception and colour perception. On Rhapsody, which chose always to dress in dimness, the last two were obliterated almost to the point of extinction, even under the conditions of illumination extant in the towns, because neither can function properly except in *bright* light. This threw emphasis on the primary sense of dark/light separation, which was even further emphasised by the fact that the people of Rhapsody chose to live a large fraction of their lives in the shadow rather than the light. In addition, of course, the inhibition of the overall sense-category of sight put a heavier responsibility on hearing (or, to be strictly accurate, on loudness perception—hearing, also, is a compound sense).

The reordering of the usefulness of my senses was an inevitability, while I was forced to operate within this environment. But changes in one's sensory orientation can sometimes result in changes in one's personality—even in one's identity. It was not so much that I feared a permanent change—I would have to spend a considerable period on Rhapsody before I became irrevocably colour-blind—but that I was worried about Grainger-on-Rhapsody behaving in a manner which might be considered aberrant by Grainger-off-Rhapsody. It was a syndrome I had encountered before on many of the worlds to which Lapthorn and I had taken the *Fire-Eater* and the *Javelin*. I had always fought such effects tooth and nail, but I had also been able to study the total subjection to them by their expression in Lapthorn, who believed in the whole experience of alien worlds. On dark worlds, he became a dark Lapthorn, on odorous worlds, an odorous Lapthorn. He *changed*, from world to world. It was not insanity, although several of his multiple forms behaved in a manner which would have been grossly out of place *everywhere else*. The syndrome is purely a matter of adaptation, but if it begins to come easily and naturally, then eventually one adaptation or another will claim one's soul, and one is trapped in an alien (alien, that is, to *other* men) environment for the rest of one's days.

It happens to a lot of spacemen. It would have happened to Lapthorn, in time, had not the crash ended his life. But it wasn't going to happen to me. I was determined never to surrender myself to alien worlds, alien ways, alien points of view.

And not to alien parasites, either.

I got up, and went out of the shack. The light was still steady and silver, and I was grateful for having found it. There was nobody around except for the lanky man—Tob—who had helped to bring me here. He was sitting just outside the door of Bayon's house, reclining with his head and shoulders supported by a cushion or rock, looking suspiciously like a jailer. He was cleaning his fingernails with a sheath-knife and he didn't bother to look up as I emerged.

"Bout time,' he murmured.

'Where is everybody?' I asked.

'We got a living to earn,' he said. 'Just 'cause you sleep till evening is no reason for us to do the same. A free life is no easy life. We have to eat. Food supply has to be kept up. That means taking stuff from the converters. It also means putting stuff back in. Them machines is about clapped. As it is, we got to get regular supplies of green-stuff from outside. Muck that grows here is no good at all. Jellied rock and glued-up dirt. We daren't just steal from the converters without putting nothing back.'

'I'm sure that your sense of social responsibility is both highly developed and highly commendable,' I said. 'Why aren't you out earning *your* living?'

'I'm baby-sitting.'

'Alpart was worried in case I woke up crying? He thought I might need something?'

'Bayon always worries.'

'That's no doubt why he boasts about his optimism. Did he think I was likely to run away?'

He looked up from his manicure, for the first time. He had a very unhandsome face, but it wasn't unfriendly. His paleness and his wispy, stunted beard made him grotesque to my eyes, but it was a face with definite humanity. So many of the faces here were white masks, with as much in-built capacity for expression as the faces of reptiles.

'You ain't very pretty,' he said, 'but we love you anyway. You mean a lot to us and we're going to look after you as well as we can.'

'Very kind of you. But you don't need to keep me a prisoner. I'm on your side.'

'Them as plays it safe,' he said, 'is the ones who manage to get by down here.'

'Them as plays it safe,' I mimicked, 'don't get kicked out of the holy flock to begin with.'

'We all make mistakes,' he said, without rancour. 'It makes us extra careful about making any more. The first mistake we made cost us our chance to live like worms. If we make the mistake of losing you it could cost us our chance to live like people.'

'Perfect,' I said. 'I can see that Bayon's got you all convinced. I know it would be no good my telling you that you probably wouldn't find the star-worlds any more accommodating than this hell-hole, and it would make me very unpopular if I did. But you don't know what the star-worlds are like. They're wonderful— but for star people.'

'Once a worm, always a worm,' he said. 'Is that what you're trying to tell me?'

'No, Tob, definitely not that. You're no worm or you wouldn't be here. You'd be in the mines or at the bottom of a hotshaft pretending to be charcoal. You can find a life in the star-worlds— I'm as sure as you are of that. What I'm trying to tell you is that it won't be easy. It won't descend upon you automatically, the minute you step onto alien soil. There will be no miracles. It'll require just the same effort and determination you put into living down here.'

'I know,' he said. Just that, without protest or emphasis. He did know. I had to stop assuming that the people of Rhapsody were ignorant savages. They were something weird all right, but it was something a lot different from naiveté and barbarity.

'Sure,' I said, 'you know. And I can't really blame you for keeping eyes on me all the time.'

'No,' he agreed, 'you can't. We need you, spaceman, a hell of a lot more than you need us.'

'My name's Grainger,' I said.

'Grainger,' he said tonelessly. 'You told us. Ain't much different from "spaceman", is it? Bayon is Bayon and I'm Tob. What's your real name?'

I sighed. 'I haven't got another name. I was born an orphan. Grainger's as real a name as I've got.'

He looked at me steadily. 'Nobody gets born an orphan,' he

said, accurately, but missing the meaning of what I'd said. 'In any case, even the orphans round here got names. They're easy to come by.'

'I don't come from around here,' I pointed out. 'It doesn't matter anyhow. I'm sorry, but I haven't got another name. I'm just Grainger, that's all.'

'Difficult to be friendly then,' he commented.

'I won't take it to be unfriendly if you call me by my name,' I assured him.

He shrugged.

'I will get you off if I can,' I told him. 'I meant what I said. If it's humanly possible, I won't leave you to die down here.'

'And this Charlot,' he said. 'The one *you* have to ask. What about him? Does he feel the same way?'

That was a very difficult question. I didn't like Charlot and he didn't like me. He didn't owe me any favours. I could hardly make promises on his behalf. On the other hand, if I expressed any doubt, or even evaded the question, I would destroy any faith which Tob might place in me. I was reasonably sure that I could get Bayon's sixteen men onto the *Hooded Swan*, but reasonably sure wasn't nearly enough for Tob and Bayon. They'd been offered the carrot, and nothing was going to stand in their way.

'Whether Charlot gets what he wants or not,' I told him, 'he'll have lots of empty space on the ship. He's a human being, like the rest of us. He couldn't possibly elect to leave you here.'

All of which must have sounded to Tob like: 'I'm not sure.'

'It's not impossible to get off the world,' I said. 'Rion Mavra and six others left.'

'Churchmen,' he said. 'Just arguers, not throwouts.'

'Yes, but ships do arrive and take off. Not just the Splinter ships, but ships to and from Attalus. Not often, I know. But there are ships. If the locals ignore you, and refuse to recognise your presence, you shouldn't have too much difficulty getting to the offworlders.'

'Do you honestly think we ain't tried?'

'No,' I said. 'I imagined you had. What goes wrong?'

'The ships that come here from outside come to deal with the Churchmen. And that isn't easy. They wouldn't do it if they didn't have to. But from time to time, Attalus wants something and only our prices are low enough. The Church wouldn't deal either, but *they* have to, as well. We couldn't live here without support. Things break. Things have to be repaired and replaced. But the Church has a choice and Attalus doesn't. Attalus needs the Church more than the Church needs Attalus. We can always trade with the companies, because we have metal we don't want, and can pay their prices.

'So do you really think that any ship from Attalus would dare to carry back renegades from Rhapsody or any other of the Splinters? They take the exiles, sure, because that's where the Church reckons its exiles ought to go. But we're dead. We don't exist, but we can't be allowed to escape from our non-existence. If we could get back our existence, the threat of excommunication would be only a tenth of what it is. The Churchmen would kill us, whether we exist or not. And the ships from Attalus wouldn't carry us. They wouldn't dare.'

I could see his point. Attalus *did* need its tenuous connection with the Splinters more than the Splinters did. It was apparent nonsense to think of Attalus being poorer than the Splinters, but that was the reality. Rhapsody had a minimum of wealth, but what it had was surplus to requirements. It could be used, in time of need. But all the wealth which Attalus possessed was tied up in maintaining a reasonable standard of living. They had much more in the way of resources, but they needed every last gram. Wealth and poverty are both determined by what is *enough*. The standard of everyday life on Rhapsody would be intolerable by the standards of Attalus.

There must be company ships as well—few and far between but I knew better than to ask Tob about that. Company men were company men. If you couldn't pay the fare, you didn't get the ride. That had been brought home to me so hard that I'd never ever forget it. Bayon, Tob and the rest were trapped—caught in the Church's web and condemned to the Church's version of hell. A living hell, where they served as terrible reminders to the faithful. The imaginary non-existence was cruel and brilliant. The people knew, but they could not admit that they knew. They lived alongside their hell, and it was an act of faith not to see it. It was even an act of faith *not to be a part of it*, for life on Rhapsody couldn't be objectively much different for the faithful and the condemned. I never found out what kind of Exclusive Reward the people were promised for their suffering—in all probability they weren't allowed to know the details, but had to take it on trust that it would be *good*—but they earned every bit of it.

They deserved it all. Their life, their heaven, and their hell. The only ones who didn't deserve it were the ones who had to suffer most—the hellbound themselves.

I meant to get them out. I really was absolutely determined. How much could I blame them for a lack of trust? Not at all, *then*. Later events cast a different shadow, though.

And what are you going to get out of it? demanded the wind.

I didn't bother with the question. His speaking had just reminded me of something.

'Last night,' I subvocalised, 'did you knock me out?'

How could I do that?

'I didn't ask how.'

You went to sleep.

'I don't usually go to sleep like somebody handed me a pile-driver on the back of the head.'

You said yourself that you were tired.

He was taunting me deliberately. So many times before, he'd assured me that he couldn't take command of my body unless I let him. But how much control did he really have? Was he really unable to act, or was he simply trying to attain his ends by guile instead of force? After all, he had to live with me. Diplomacy made a lot of sense.

I didn't knock you out, he said suddenly.

I couldn't tell whether it was because the joke was over, or whether it was because he didn't like the way my train of thought was taking me.

'I don't believe you,' I said.

It's true. I cannot render you unconscious by any direct action. I cannot subvert any voluntary control which you have over your body. I did not knock you unconscious last night.

There was nothing to be gained by further argument. I had to accept what he said, or else reject it outright without any real evidence. I accepted it, but retained my doubts. I returned my attention to Tob.

'What happens when they get back? And when is that likely to be?'

'Pretty soon,' he said. 'You slept most of the day anyway. And when they come back we'll be eating. After that, I guess we'll be moving. Bayon won't want to waste any more time. Once we've laid in the supplies, we'll be on our way.'

'Revolution time,' I said. 'All sixteen of you.'

'Ain't no law against it,' he said.

'True,' I conceded. And it was true, in more than a meta-phorical sense. Fomenting revolution was against the Law of New Rome. If I had been on any planet other than an LWA I'd be risking twenty years (despite the fact that I wasn't actually fomenting anything—you know what the Law's like).

The prospect of action gladdened me. I wasn't really in favour of the tough line, although I admitted its potential, but I really did need something to *do*. Another time, another place, I could maybe have sat down and waited forever, lying in a hammock drowsing in the sunlight. But Rhapsody dressed exclusively in black, and sitting here was far too much like sitting in a coffin. Lying down was a declaration of intent to die. I needed some-thing to occupy me, body and soul.

Something other than the wind.

A life of my own. I'd already had a taste of eternal death two years of it on Lapthorn's Grave, where there was nothing to do except stand that bloody cross up two or three times a day. Well, the cross was down now, no doubt, and it would stay down forever.

And that's how and why I became Rhapsody's public enemy number one.

CHAPTER ELEVEN

Right from the start I was plagued by the suspicion that the boss wasn't cut out for his job. It all seemed horribly familiar. Nick delArco was a good guy but he was no starship captain. Bayon Alpart was the natural leader of his band, but he was operating on a scale that he couldn't handle. You can't just *be* a hero, or a gangster, or a revolutionary, or a tough guy. You have to have the qualifications. They don't hand out bits of paper for those things even in the weirdest of academies. But the bits of paper are all fakes anyhow. The qualifications are inside you, but they don't just grow there—they have to be put there.

Bayon didn't really know what he was doing or how he was going to do it. But he couldn't admit that, because he was the boss and bosses can't doubt. Maybe I shouldn't cry too loudly, because I probably couldn't have done any better. I didn't have the qualifications either. But that still didn't make me happy. I couldn't question his strategy, his intentions, his methods or his chances. There was no *obvious* road to where we wanted to go. And it was his party. I was only along for the ride. An extra card in his hand, an extra weapon for his fight. The fact that he was a local boy who knew only the Rhapsody angle and I was a worldly-wise citizen of the galaxy was only a fact, not an argument. He had the greater subjectivity; I had the greater objectivity. There was no way of knowing which talent might solve the problem. I had no real kick. I was one of the gang and that was it. No hero, no war leader, no expert. I had to play my role from behind.

Frankly, I was scared. Things could go wrong. And when things go wrong during gun-toting operations, people can get hurt. *Very* hurt. Personally, I don't like guns. I volunteered not to carry one (we had more men than guns). But I didn't imagine that would make it any less likely that I'd get shot if the bullets and the beams actually started to fly.

The first difficulty we had to cope with, of course, was gaining access to the grotto without giving advance warning or having to cope with any extra bother *en route*. Naturally enough, we didn't have a map. Most civilisations are flat and can be mapped flat. Rhapsody wasn't and couldn't. The problem of approach and access was a problem in three-dimensional geometry and dispersion. The grotto, of course, was only a single point on a single line. It was the intersections of the other lines which disobeyed good two-dimensional sense.

The problem was simple. We wanted to preserve a way out without conceding the opposition a way in. The disposition of sixteen men to achieve this end required very difficult thinking. I couldn't get near it. All that had to be trusted to Bayon's judgement. He did try to explain, but it was pointless, and I had to tell him so. I knew a bit about arterial and venous shafts, about towers and showers, and about the anatomy of alveolar systems. But only a bit. The pattern of tunnelling imposed by the necessity for supporting the rock was beyond me, and I didn't know the territory involved.

The outcasts had spent the whole day in stockpiling food and water. Their raiding expedition must itself have been a strategic masterpiece. They had stolen enough gruel to last sixteen of us a week. There was less water than would last us half that long, but the area we intended to command included several sources—and there was always the additional chance that the cave we intended to take contained water.

I wondered what was going on back at the capital, in the meantime. Had the council made a decision? If so, then we might be sticking our heads in the lion's mouth. If the booty was already committed to Sampson, he and his crew would be quite prepared to shoot their way in to claim it, and the Churchmen would be prepared to let them. If Charlot had acquired title, which was more likely, the prospects were a lot better. We'd hand it over and help him load it up in exchange for a ride out and—dare I hold out for it?—a small payment to save time and guarantee exclusive rights.

On the other hand, if the council had not yet handed on their hot potato, they might be prepared to attach conditions about dealing with outcasts—like, for instance, Charlot would only get the goods if he guaranteed to leave the hellbound in hell. That possibility would almost certainly lead to trouble.

And, in further complication, there was also the awkward little fact that Charlot had yet to pay me back for the *Lost Star* doublecross. How that was going to affect matters, Charlot alone could tell.

The outcasts were quite relaxed, considering the importance of the operation. When Bayon detailed his plans and handed out the jobs, they nodded calmly and the questions they asked were confined to matters of importance. There was no sign of doubt or frayed nerves. Nobody was looking for trouble; everybody would be ready for it if it came. They all gave the appearance of being strong, capable men. But then, they had been selected by the rigorous process of survival.

We moved off just as soon as we had finished talking. There was no zero hour set for dramatic purposes. We got ready, and when we were ready, we went. We split into groups as men peeled away from the main group in order to adopt their specific positions defending our potential escape route from any surrounding operation mounted by the enemy.

The eventual assault party was just five strong. There was Bayon, Tob, two men named Harl and Ezra, and myself. Bayon carried the best of his group's weapons—their solitary power rifle. It was only about half charged, but you can cause an awful lot of mayhem with a half charged beam gun. At a reasonable rate of power-release it could burn a hole through a couple of hundred men, if they were obliging enough to stand in a straight line so that no power splashed astray. Tob, Harl and Ezra were all armed with ordinary projectile weapons. The main advantage of a standard gun over a beamer is range, and so we were ill-armed for our purposes. The three rifles were by no means primitive—they were good, efficient pieces of machinery, whose design had been perfected centuries before. But their *presence* on Rhapsody was a little incongruous, let alone their prevalence over the beam guns which the inhabitants would have found much more functional in the general run of their affairs. But the people of Rhapsody were far from immune from the small illogicalities which invariably plague dogmatically maintained cultures. The Church of the Exclusive Reward had armed itself only to answer the possibility that they might be called upon to defend their isolation and alienation. They were not an armed society by nature. Possibly, they had chosen to employ so few beamers *because* the power of such weapons was so immoderate and ubiquitous.

We made our approach via a network of bleak, difficult passages, which seemed to bend about themselves tortuously. To my (admittedly uneducated) eye they did not look to be alveolar vessels at all, but faults caused at some distant time past by stress within the alveolar architecture. My flashlight had not yet been exhausted, but I used it very sparingly, saving as much light as I could for the indeterminate future. Bayon and his men, as was usual, showed no dislike for the darkness, and moved with ample confidence therein. Occasionally, though—when it was necessary to avoid deep pits or pass by loose structures of rock which threatened disaster if disturbed—even Bayon expressed gratitude for the availability of light. He had his own lanterns, of course, but he was as jealous of these as I was with the light of my flash. Conservation was always his first priority. I had to be given frequent help in the tunnels, but Tob was ever-present and discreet, so that I did not make too much of a fool of myself.

The worst part of the journey by far was the ascent of a slanting hotshaft which was only ten or fifteen degrees from the vertical.

Here, fortunately, we had light in plenty—not just from the flash and Bayon's lamps, but from the walls themselves, where luminous life-forms clung to the scattered crevices which we used for handholds. Thus, not only was our way lighted but we knew where to reach for with both hands and toes by the brightness of the light. The climb was rendered practical by virtue of this coincidence. Without the organisms, the danger of slipping down the shaft while we manipulated our own lights to our convenience would have been considerable, and we would probably have had to choose another way to the grotto. And there was no other way available which offered us such a close approach without the danger of interception.

The shaft disgorged us into a corridor about four feet tall and three across, through which we had to crawl for a hundred metres before emerging into a vertical slit, where we paused for the first time. The slit opened directly into the blind mine-shaft where the grotto was situated.

We had presumed that there would be no guards beyond the opening of the slit, since they would only be covering limited access. This implied that we had only to contend with those who were now between ourselves and our objective.

Harl and Tob went on, easing themselves out into the shaft. Tob went right, to check our hypothesis that there were no guards that way. Harl went left, to find out how many we had to deal with at the mouth of the grotto.

We waited anxiously, wooing the silence and dreading the sound of shots from either direction.

Three minutes elapsed before Harl came back.

'Two,' he said, and Bayon heaved a sigh of relief. Had there been more, the likelihood of a battle would have increased greatly. Two men are a partnership, and may be expected to behave sensibly. Three make a crowd, and cannot.

We had to wait a further three minutes for Tob. His task had taken longer, because he was looking for something which was (as we had hoped) not there.

'What's the light like at the cave-mouth?' Bayon asked.

'Two masked lanterns. Purely a formality. They can't do much,' supplied Harl.

'Good. Take it dead slow. No noise. Wait until we're all in a firing position—we'll have to feel our way.'

'Right,' said Tob.

'You know what to say?' Bayon addressed me.

'Sure,' I said. It had to be me who did the talking. We didn't want any silliness about problems of existence and recognition of same.

The muted lanterns were all in our favour. It might be expected that if they were bothering to guard something, the miners would also have made provision for the guards to get a clear sight down the tunnel for a few metres, at least. But that wasn't Rhapsody's way. Tunnel creatures shun the light.

And so we were allowed to make our approach in deep shadow, unseen and unsuspected.

We had expected the guards to be at ease—off their guard, in fact—since their presence there was largely symbolical, and they were prevented by lack of light from doing any effective guarding. But we were wrong. This pair were taking it seriously, without realising the incongruity. They were standing straight, rifles at the ready, alert for any sound. The light of masked lamps made them easy targets, but I don't think they realised that fact. Unless, of course, they were merely putting on a show.

Which was entirely possible, because as we arranged ourselves into a line preparatory to attack, we realised that somebody else was inside the grotto. If there were more guards, with more guns, the situation was much worse than we had thought.

We could hear voices, but we couldn't hear what was being said, so they didn't give us any clue to the identity of the people inside.

We all knew what was going on, but we couldn't start a discussion about it. We were far too close for a whisper not to carry. I didn't dare start my spiel, ordering the guards to drop their guns, in case there were more guns inside and the people holding them were alerted. For the same reason, I hoped Bayon would decide against shooting down the sentries. That narrow entrance could be defended from the inside for a considerable time. Lives would be lost in taking the grotto on those terms.

The only course left open to us, it seemed to me, was to try stealth and speed simultaneously, and hope to succeed by surprise. I couldn't tell Bayon so, and I couldn't act myself, because I didn't have a gun. So I just stood there, and waited for our noble leader to do his stuff.

CHAPTER TWELVE

Bayon was in no hurry. He elected to wait and watch. In this case, his judgement proved superior to mine. Within a few minutes, they came out of the grotto.

There were four of them. One I didn't know and one I couldn't see. The other two were Rion Mavra and Cyolus Capra. The four of them were engaged in a conversation—whose content we still could not identify. They paused just outside the entrance to the grotto so that the leading man—the one I didn't know—could emphasise some point he was making.

I felt Bayon tense as he levelled his gun, but he still held back and allowed them to come on.

Mavra and the unknown man moved forward together, and the others dropped back, apparently temporarily disengaged from the conversation. I saw the fourth figure highlighted briefly beyond and between Mavra and the other. It was Angelina. The surprise was momentary—I couldn't afford the time to think about it.

Then Bayon moved.

Involved as they were with one another, neither man saw us as we covered the three paces which separated us. They reacted only when violent hands were laid upon them.

Bayon reached out to take Mavra's head in the crook of his arm, and swung the smaller man around effortlessly. Mavra gasped, but he was drowned by Bayon's loud yell.

'Ezra! Get Krist! Tob the other one! Grainger the girl.'

The allocation of tasks did not represent any denigration of my fighting spirit relative to his own men, but merely reflected the way we had lined up. We were already halfway to completing what Bayon demanded of us.

Ezra took hold of the man that I had not recognised—Akim Krist, it seemed—and shoved him into the wall of the tunnel, moving in behind him so that Krist's body shielded him from the armed men, while his own rifle was aligned across Krist's chest in a threatening position.

Meanwhile, Bayon had gone forward, moving Mavra with him as a human shield.

Capra had moved instinctively backward and to one side, and it was not necessary for Tob to clear him out of Bayon's way. But Angelina froze, and I had to lunge forward, lift her bodily, and then force her right down, so that Ezra and Harl could—if necessary—fire over our bodies. Chivalrously, I fell on top of her instead of getting underneath her so that she would absorb any loose lead. I think it was an accident—it was the way we fell.

The guards had acted with all due suddenness in levelling their guns and striking an aggressive pose. Mercifully, though, they were not so trigger-conscious as to let fly without a decent amount of premeditation. Sensibly, they didn't fire at all.

There was a sudden and profound silence. I caught myself waiting for something to happen, and remembered that I was the mouthpiece.

'Put the guns down,' I said levelly.

The guards hesitated. Their exaggerated trepidation clearly showed that they recognised Bayon, who was only a few feet away, staring at them over Mavra's head. But it was quite clear that the Hierarch himself, Akim Krist, was convinced of the reality of the gun which held him pinned to the wall, and he was having no trouble compromising with the unreality of its holder.

'Tell 'em, Krist,' growled Ezra, relishing the menace in his own voice. Heroically, Krist ignored him.

I released Angelina, leaving her huddled on the ground. I brushed past the trailing arm of the prisoned Mavra and walked up to the guards. They looked at me with distaste, but they had already relaxed the attitude of their guns. I secured both rifles, and used them to point the way into the grotto. Both guards accepted the invitation, and descended the short slope into the glittering interior of the treasure cave.

I turned around, bowed slightly, and gestured to the grotto with my empty hand. My eyes met Mavra's. His gaze was colourless, lacking both surprise and reproach. Krist, however, had realised that I was solid, and was regarding me with mixed hatred and anger. His eyes were fixed on me, as he refused to honour my companions with the direction of his stare.

One by one, they all filed past me into the grotto. Harl helped Angelina to her feet, and to my surprise—and his—she thanked him in a low voice. She almost smiled at me as she brushed past, but her face couldn't quite manage it. In any case, it would have been an enigmatic smile—I was reasonably sure that she was not amused, and she could hardly be making us welcome.

I was about to enter, last of all, but I had to step back to let Harl out again. After the slightest of glances around the object of our exercise he had been ordered out again by Bayon to replace the previous guardians. He carried both of our lamps, and he was taking the masks off the other lights preparatory to distributing them intelligently in the corridor when I stepped into the grotto.

It was full of light.

Even so, there was no glare. The light was faint and filmy, like the light of the Milky Way as seen from a rim world on a clear night. It was an oddly familiar and—to me—beautiful effect. The floor had been cleared to leave a short pathway and a square space in the centre of the cave, which was just adequate to accommodate the ten of us. Standing room only.

The grotto was shaped like a cone with the point lopped off, but the interior surface was knobbed and distorted, with abundant rock-forms like stalagmites and stalactites. It looked to be a stress-cyst rather than an alveolar pocket. Its base diameter was about five metres, but the walls sloped inwards, tapering so that at eye-height the grotto only seemed to be about three metres wide.

The entire inner surface except for the patch where we stood was encrusted with blue-grey and green-grey growths which had luminescent facets set in ordered array over their tegument, like tiny sequins.

There was a small semicircular pool in the rear of the cave. Its surface was jet black, but set with a multitude of very faint pinpricks which were the reflections of the facets in the water. Beside the pool was an irregular heap of randomly lighted debris—obviously the detritus which had been cleared to allow spectators the room to stand.

'Very nice,' I commented.

Bayon and his men were strangely wary, now that the action was over. They were looking about suspiciously, trying to see something which might be worth all this fuss. But there was nothing which could even seem unfamiliar to them.

'It's gone!' said Ezra.

'No it hasn't,' I told him. 'This little collection we've assembled didn't come here for the privacy. And no one guards empty caves. It's still here, whatever it is.'

I wanted to get a close look, but it was impossible with the crowd crammed into the small cleared space.

'Get them out,' I said to Bayon. 'They're in the way.'

'You'll have to tell them,' he reminded me.

I located Rion Mavra and addressed myself to him. 'Look,' I said. 'If we're going to be difficult about this, there's going to be a lot of unnecessary tension generated. Do you think that you could possibly admit—temporarily—that those guns have trigger-fingers on them, and that the men with the trigger-fingers should be obeyed?'

'We'll do as you say, of course,' said Mavra, without committing himself.

'Well then, I'll put you in charge of liaison. If my wishes aren't carried out, one of you might get shot by some nasty non-existent person. I want you all out of here and into the blind end of the mine-workings. I want you to imagine that there's a guard with you watching your every move. This imaginary guard will be called Ezra, if you wish to imagine that you can talk to him for the purpose of asking for something. I want you to make yourselves as comfortable as possible and wait. Do you think that you can handle all those instructions in one go?'

'We'll do as you say. But I'd like to talk to you about what you're trying to do.'

'Capture your big prize,' I said, waving an arm about my head (with some difficulty) to indicate the span of my ambitions.

'What do you hope to gain by taking by force what your employer might well get by honest means?' he followed up.

'Ah, well, there's the rub,' I said. 'It's not primarily what I want which brought me here. I'm looking after the interests of some other people. You might not know them, though I'm sure you could if you made the effort. It would save you from having to assume that it was the will of God which picked you up in the corridor and brought you back in here.'

He didn't seem impressed.

'Do you intend to hold us as hostages?'

'Bayon?' I asked.

'Yes,' said Bayon.

'Yes,' I repeated, playing the game. 'Now get out and do as I told you. Ezra, sit them down in a neat little group. If they don't know what you want them to do, hint by means of a few swift kicks. I think they'll catch on. We'll come back to them in a few minutes, when I've had a look around.'

They all filed out, and a sudden afterthought sent me out into the tunnel after them.

'By the way,' I said, tapping Mavra on the shoulder, 'you wouldn't care to tell me what to look for, I suppose?'

It was Angelina who answered. 'I'm sure, Captain Grainger, that you have sufficient intelligence to see what is before you.'

It was the first time she'd spoken in my presence, and the heavy irony startled me. 'I'm not the captain,' I said. 'I only fly the ship.'

'What about you?' said Ezra to Akim Krist. The Hierarch ignored him—looked straight through him.

'Capra?' I asked.

'There's nothing in there,' he said, with a grotesquely ineffective attempt at defiance.

'Ah, forget it,' I addressed them collectively. 'I'll find out for myself.' And I returned to the grotto to do just that.

There were three types of organism.

The primary producer was the luminescent organism. It was—quite literally—the base element of the system. It spread vegetatively over the inner surface of the grotto, like a thick coat of paint. It varied in thickness from about half an inch to one-and-a-half, according to the pieces which I inspected. (I took fresh specimens from the wall rather than look at the organisms which had been cleared from the floor, in case the latter had deteriorated.) Its texture was soft and easily breakable, like a dry, firm fungus. Internally it was partially differentiated into ill-defined strata, in and between which were suspended cloud-like 'organs'. There did not seem to be any cellular structure, nor was there a multi-molecular fibrous skeleton. The differentiation seemed to be purely and simply a matter of molecular densities and protoplasmic cohesion. It was difficult to be certain with only the feeble light of my flashlight, and without any magnifier, but I formed the impression that the cloud areas were motile within the strata, and that there must be considerable streaming of molecules within the protoplasm. I noticed that as I held a plaque of the substance between my fingers, the luminescence died, but if I placed the distal surface against the palm of my hand, it grew brighter. The reaction was quick, and quite considerable for such a minor difference in temperature; it seemed obvious that the organism was thermosynthetic, gaining energy from the excitement of molecules by heat energy. The luminescence was probably an energy-excretory process— a means of disposing of absorbed energy which could not be immediately channelled into anabolic and catabolic processes.

This type of organism was representative of a class which

often developed on conductive faces near hotcores. It could not be the cause of all the excitement.

The second type consisted of certain small growths which studded the sequined carpet. Each growth looked like a tiny tree, beginning at a single point and bifurcating as each branch reached a length of two and a half inches. The branches did not grow high but remained close to the substratum, so that the dendrite proliferated mostly in a horizontal plane. Some of these organisms had attained a diameter of fifteen inches, but most were a great deal smaller.

The active elements of the organism were borne at the tip of each branch—oval, sapphire-like bodies (not luminescent) which apparently secreted the branches over a period of time, and caused a bifurcation every time they divided—presumably by ordinary binary fission. I detached one of the dendrites from its bed, and carefully inspected the material which made up the skeletal elements. It had a curious almost-metallic texture, which reminded me of something which momentarily eluded my mind. The translucent blue skin of the vital cell, coupled with the familiar form of the organism, led me to believe that it used as its energy source the light excreted by the thermosynthetic carpet. Since it was basically similar to eukaryot types which could be found on virtually every habitable world in the galaxy, I concluded that this also could not be the Great Discovery. Leaving aside the microscopic endoparasites which undoubtedly existed in the system, I was thus left with the last visible type.

This type was difficult to spot, even though I knew roughly what to look for—a secondary consumer. I expected to find some kind of motile plasmid which ate the vital cells of the dendrites, but all the dendrites I inspected had all their cells intact.

It took me some time, but I finally noticed that it was the dendritic stalks, and not the living cells, which showed evidence of attack. This was unusual. It is not uncommon, of course, for non-living structural material to be organic in content, and hence an available source of food for another organism. But these dendritic skeletons had seemed to be metallic rather than carbonaceous. I puzzled for a while over this peculiarity, wondering what it could mean, while I continued my search for the organism itself.

It was, as I'd expected, a motile form, but the specimens which I eventually located were sitting quite still, wrapped around the dendritic elements like tiny protoplasmic rings. They could be induced by a gentle prod to unwind and reveal their true nature—long, thin and vermiform.

No infected dendrite, so far as I could see, carried more than one ring, and most had none, which made the worms rare by any standard. Their total biomass couldn't be more than a couple of grams.

Since the stalks which supported the teardrop cells did not seem to me to be nourishing enough to support a reasonable standard of living, it occurred to me that the worms might also make use of the light so obligingly provided by the thermo-synths.

Accordingly, I fished out my flashlight for the second time and shone its wan glow upon one of the coiled-up worms.

Which promptly became two worms. The plasmid divided *in situ*, without uncoiling. One of the two shuffled sideways and where there had been only one ring, there were now two. The stalk had been thinned extensively during the process— corroded away as though by strong acid. The reproduction took less than a minute. I switched off the flashlight promptly, not wishing to precipitate a population explosion. The rate at which the plasmid had absorbed the light energy, sucked up the stalk material and used it to good purpose was nothing short of phenomenal. In a cave like this, of course, conditions would have been more or less stable for millions of years. The energy supply at the conductive face would be very slow and very constant. The differences in temperature with which the thermosynth mobilised its heat energy were probably minute— hence the strong reaction to my body heat, which must be very close to the temperature of the rock. The light generated under natural conditions here must have been stable in intensity for all those millions of years. The whole system was perfectly attuned, and overreacted when new stimuli were applied. Had the people of Rhapsody cut their way in here with beamers, and then leaped into the space with bright lights blazing, the delicate balance of the system would have gone completely wild, and the entire ecocomplex might have been destroyed in a matter of days. But Rhapsody's miners worked with pickaxes and without light. So the complex was still here, and would probably have sufficient resilience to take the new conditions into account and go on for ever.

But the question of its value was not yet settled.

The worms were the unique types. They were a product of split adaptation, and that *they* had evolved to balance the system rather than a more conventional secondary consumer had to be a million-to-one chance. The key to it all was in the limiting factors. The thermosynth was limited by space, not by consumption on the part of the dendrites. The dendritic cells were not limited at all except by the supply of light energy. The same factor limited the capacity of the worms to metabolise the stalks. Thus the efficiency and continuity of the system were not determined by mortality, but by the constancy of the conditions applying a restraint to natality. There were no sources of mortality external to the populations themselves.

If, therefore, the only limiting factor constraining the worms was light, and they could eat stalks *ad infinitum* given that light, take them out into the sunlight and they would eat up mountains of the stalk-stuff.

But what *was* the stalk-stuff? The living cells were at the termini of the branches, and were connected to their substratum only via a narrow canal through the centre of the dead stalk. I judged that there would be no sense in their being up there rather than embedded in the thermosynth unless they absorbed atmospheric gases, and could not afford to be overgrown by the slowly-thickening carpet. That made sense too. Luminosity usually involves oxidation. If the thermosynth was taking oxygen out of the air to make its light, something must be putting it back. So the dendrites might well take in carbon dioxide and release oxygen, in typical plant fashion. That implied the stalks contained carbon. They also contained something which was brought up from the rock via the canals. Metal. To be specific, copper.

Which implied...

All of a sudden—and belatedly, it seemed—inspiration struck home, and it all fell into place. I knew why the worms were so valuable. It wasn't mountains that they could eat, but cities.

'Obviously,' I commented drily.

I'd accidentally spoken out loud, believing that I was alone in the grotto. But Bayon had apparently been sitting in the entrance watching me for some time.

'Well,' he said. 'What is it?'

'There are three types of organism here,' I told him. I searched for simple terms which he might be able to under-stand. I couldn't hope to give him the entire picture, let alone explain my logic, but I could give him a fair idea of what was what. 'The first eats heat and gives off light. The second is like a plant. It uses the light as energy. It has stalks which are made from carbon taken out of the air and copper taken out of the rock. The third is odd. It might have started out in life trying to be another plant, but found it couldn't make it. Nor could it make it as pure animal, so it had to be both.

'It uses the light to provide energy for chewing its way through the stalks of the plant. It takes the carbon for its own structural purposes, and excretes the copper, which just gets absorbed into the thermosynthetic carpet—the luminous stuff, that is. There's a complicated circulation of oxygen and carbon dioxide in the air which keeps the whole thing balanced.'

'So what?' said Bayon. An understandable reaction.

'Well, the half-and-half creature will take all the light it can get in order to chew up the stalks. If we were to flood the cave with light, the thing would go through its total supply in a couple of days, despite the fact that there's a lot of it compared to the present number of worms. The rate of conversion is very, very fast.'

'And?' he prompted. I don't think he was following me—if he was, he certainly wasn't appreciating the sheer elegance of the system. Rhapsody as a whole was greatly lacking in aesthetic appreciation.

'The stalks are made of carbon and copper. I don't know of any way this can be done except by forming complex molecules called cupro-carbon-chains. They're extremely rare in nature on any world, but the clever old human race discovered how to synthesise the molecules long before they were identified in living tissue. Depending on the precise configuration of the molecule, cupro-carbon-chains can be very hard or quite malleable. In some families of chain, the application of heat can change the structure. This means that cupro-carbon-chains are immensely useful as building material. Cupro-carbon houses are virtually indestructible. They can be moulded hot, and then when the material cools it undergoes a reaction which makes it hard. The reaction is irreversible, and reheating has no effect. Once a cuprocarbon building is up, it stays up forever.

'Until these little worms see the light of day. You can't really envision the scale of the destruction which these little things can cause, because Rhapsody doesn't use cupro-carbon-chains any more than it uses all the other sophisticated—and expensive—methods which grew up during the last few centuries. But this stuff could destroy a civilisation, Bayon. Whole worlds of buildings. Greedily and speedily. It couldn't be stopped.'

'So that's why it's so valuable?' said Bayon.

'That,' I agreed, 'is it.'

'Then let's go back and talk to Krist and Mavra.'

'What for?'

'I want to know what's happening back at the capital.'

'What are you going to do about this?' I asked him.

'Stay with it.'

'We could grab some and go,' I pointed out.

He shook his head. 'I've got all of it and I'm keeping all of it. What little I could carry away would be worthless if the council decided to give some to Charlot *and* Sampson.'

He had a point there. We didn't actually know we had cornered the supply—any number of people might have taken some out. But Krist had brought Mavra and company down here to have a look, which *might* signify that there was none to look at back home in the capital.

I followed him back out into the mine, carrying one of the infected dendrites in my hand. Once outside, though, I remembered what the lantern light could do to it, and I threw it back.

Then, with Bayon feeding me some of the questions, I began the interrogation.

'How many people know about this?' I addressed the question to Mavra, since he seemed most likely to answer.

'Too many,' he replied, a little gloomily.

'Do Charlot and Sampson know what it is?'

'Do you?' he countered, checking to make sure that I wasn't trying to bluff him.

'It eats cities,' I said. 'And I know how, too.'

He shook his head slightly, but it wasn't a denial. He was just lamenting the state of the game. 'I don't think they know yet,' he said. 'Although I don't know what Gimli might have told Sampson. But it's only a matter of time. We can't keep the secret. Word not only leaked offplanet, but even out of the Splinters. Charlot has to find out soon.'

'Gimli tried to set up a deal with Sampson for his own benefit, is that right?'

'Not only Gimli. Several men made some kind of attempt to make a private fortune. Gimli was the most important. But too many people knew. They all got in one another's way. There might have been murder if the miners hadn't been armed in order to control the situation. Now it's a matter for the council.'

'Who armed the miners?'

'Krist and others. They wouldn't have acted without the

knowledge of the Hierarch.'

'What is the council going to do?'

He shrugged again. 'I shudder to think. Unless you release us, they might go ahead without us. Without the Hierarch, they could decide almost anything. And there's likely to be more trouble when you do release us. We're no good to you as hostages—you'd lose nothing by letting us go.'

'That's what they all say,' I commented. 'Bayon?'

'I'm not letting them go,' he said definitely.

'They'll kill you for sure if you kill Krist,' I reminded him. 'And they probably don't care much either way about Mavra and the others. I don't think they really give you much extra bargaining power'

'They stay,' he repeated. 'Ask Krist what he wanted to do with the grotto, if not to make his own fortune'

I repeated the question, but Krist wouldn't reply. Either he had decided that I had been contaminated by theoretical non-existence, or he was just stubborn.

'Well,' I said, 'it can only really be one of two things. Either he wants to promote the discovery for the mutual benefit of all the lucky people on Rhapsody, Ecstasy, Serenity, Vitality, Modesty, Felicity, Fidelity, Harmony and Sanctity, or he wants to close up the grotto and bury the whole problem. Since he's the Church Hierarch, I suspect it's the latter. Politically unpopular but doctrinally safe.' All the time, I was looking at Krist, hoping for a reaction.

But it was Angelina who reacted. She laughed.

'Not at all, *Mister* Grainger. You misjudged our beloved spiritual leader. He didn't bring us down here to give us a lecture on the spirit of our noble people, and how it must be preserved at all cost by banishing this evil power from our lives. He was trying to persuade us to quite a different point of view. He wishes to adopt this gift from the Almighty and use it for the purpose which the Almighty probably had in mind. He thinks the discovery of the grotto is a commission from heaven to go and exact just retribution for all the sins that galactic civilisation has committed since we left them to tread our path of exclusive holiness.'

'If you talk like that all the time, it's no wonder they threw you out,' I said absently, while I contemplated the import of what she had told me. Krist was some fanatic if he thought his mission in life was to bring a new and terrible plague into the galaxy. This was a dangerous man.

'And you want Akim Krist back at the head of the council when they decide!' I said to Mavra. 'Do you go for this lunacy as well?'

'Quite the reverse,' he said dully. 'My fear was that if the council finds out that you're holding the Hierarch at gunpoint, they might decide that all outworlders *are* vermin, to be stamped out. It'll help his cause, not hinder it.'

'*I'm* not holding him at gunpoint,' I protested. 'I'm only here to help out. It wasn't my idea.'

'Don't you see?' said Angelina. 'The *council* is only going to see *you*. Bayon and the others don't exist. Even Rion Mavra hasn't consented to see them yet, let alone the Hierarch and this other fool. You may not be in control of the situation here but *you're going to get the blame*. Can't you see that?'

I could see it all right, but it was far too late.

'Bayon,' I said intensely, 'you've got to let them go.'

I turned to face him, and found that the gun he held was pointed at me as well.

'No,' he said.

CHAPTER THIRTEEN

What now, little man? said the wind.

I wished that I knew.

I wasn't a prisoner, exactly, but Bayon had made it pretty clear that he was calling the tune, and I'd better not forget it.

We moved away down the corridor, past the entrance where Harl and Tob stood guard, so that we could discuss things like rational human beings.

'Bayon,' I said, 'we've got to destroy the grotto.'

He looked at me as if I were crazy.

'Take some of it back to your village, but destroy whatever we leave behind,' I followed up. 'Then you still have the possibility of a deal.'

'As long as I have all of it,' he said, 'what does it matter where it is?'

'You're setting me up, Bayon. The Churchmen are going to blame me, just as Angelina says. They're not going to be disposed to make a reasonable deal with anybody while there's an outworlder holding the grotto with the Hierarch as his hostage. Take some, destroy the rest and let them go. Mavra's not against us. He's with Charlot. He'll set up a deal for us. That's what you need, if you're going to get out. As things are, they might send the miners in with the guns, or even deal with Sampson on condition he brings the guns in.'

'They won't send any guns in while we have Akim Krist.'

'But what do you think you're trying to do?' I complained. 'What chain of events are you hoping for? I don't see your thinking at all.'

'I want whatever I can get. I want off this world. I don't care who takes me. But that's not all—not any more. I've got more than just the grotto. I've got Akim Krist as well. Which means that the *Church*, as well as the offworlders, is going to deal with *me*. Before I say goodbye for good, I'm going to force them to recognise my existence. Krist and Gimli and all the rest. They're going to remember Bayon Alpart. They're going to remember that he exists; and that he's alive and well.

'It's not a matter of revenge, Grainger, believe me. It's a matter of principle. I want them all to admit they were in the wrong. I want them to see me—and what they did to me— whether they want to or not. And you needn't worry about your taking all the blame. I'm claiming that for myself. Everybody is going to *know* who stole their treasure. And to make sure that they remember, I'm taking the price of the grotto as well. All of it. The Church men won't get a penny. Nothing.'

'They won't let you get away with that!' I protested. 'Hell, there are only sixteen of you.'

'We have Akim Krist'

'You have a very inflated idea of Akim Krist's worth'

'You don't understand,' he said. 'Akim Krist is the Hierarch of Rhapsody. The leader of the Church.'

'Only on this world. And even here, he isn't an absolute monarch. He's just not that important. Remember, it's Gimli we have to negotiate with now. The man who wanted to sell out the world, just as you do. You'll never get away with it. You'll get us all killed.'

'I'm dead already, remember.'

'Well, I'm not, and I don't want to be. If this plan of yours doesn't work—and it won't—I'm right out on a limb. It's all very well for you to take the blame—but if it goes wrong, that's so much extra blame for *me* to take.'

'That's right! You just keep thinking about that, and do your level best to make sure things come out the way *I* want them to.

'This is what I'm going to do. I'm going to send the two

miners back to the capital. You can give them a message to take to Gimli. I want him down here, alone, first thing in the morning. My men will let him in provided he's alone, and we'll let him out again afterwards. But don't mention my men. Make things easy for him to begin with. Just let them tell him that he can get in and out provided that he doesn't bring any guns with him. Right?'

I did as he asked. What else could I do? But I was very unhappy about the state of affairs. Mere hours ago, I thought that the principle of Let Well Alone was a convenience, because it meant I could dabble in revolution without breaking the Law. But it also meant, of course, that the locals could shoot me down with a similar degree of safety. There was no justice.

I settled down on the bare rock, to sleep. Bayon and his three followers were sleeping in shifts. Mavra, Capra and Angelina had also decided to sleep, but Akim Krist was still wide awake, with his eyes gleaming in the lamplight as he radiated his anger.

I found that I didn't want to sleep. It had, after all, been mid-afternoon when I last awoke.

Never mind, said the wind. If Bayon does scoop the jackpot he might give you twenty thousand for your help. Then you can say goodbye to Charlot and join the gang for good.

'Bayon's worse than Charlot.'

Poor Grainger! Everybody pushes him around. But on the other hand, who would you rather have win the deal, Bayon or Akim Krist?

'Neither of them, damn it. Nor do I particularly want Charlot or Sampson putting it to all the uses their horrible imaginations might conceive. The grotto ought to be destroyed.'

That's very noble of you. I thought you were in this solely for the profit. I didn't realise you wanted to save the galaxy from the terrible scourge.

'To tell you the truth,' I said, 'if it was a choice between making twenty thousand to buy my life back and saving the galaxy, I'd probably take the twenty thousand. But I wouldn't like doing it'

How very kind. I'm sure the galaxy would thank you for your regret.

'Well, it's a redundant question anyhow. From here and now, I'd like to see the thing destroyed. My chances of getting twenty thousand out of this are comfortably outweighed by my chances of getting killed. I'll settle for nothing and a chance to go home. If I could get that power-gun off Bayon I could burn up every damned worm in the grotto in a matter of minutes. That's all it takes. We could kill the whole farce stone dead. Then I could quietly lift the *Swan*—with Bayon's sixteen as passengers—and we could all live happily ever after.'

Everything back to square one. What a way to exploit opportunity. Here's something unique in human experience, and all you want is to kill it and live happily ever after. Suppose the human who figured out how to use fire had thought like that?

'If I thought that humans had any common sense I'd say that the first fifty who thought of it did just that. But most of us have about as much sense as Akim Krist or Bayon. They're never satisfied with what they can get. They want the moon as well.'

At least they want to do *something*. It may not be the right thing, by your thinking, but it's positive. And what's wrong with Charlot's answer—New Alexandria gets the bug, which is a lot safer for all concerned than someone like Krist, or even Sampson, getting it. And the Splinters—Rhapsody at least— get the help they need to restore themselves to the human scale of existence.

'They chose to live here. They still choose to do so. They don't want that kind of help and nobody should try to force it down their throats. And as for New Alexandria being any better than Star Cross or anyone else—that's just not true. The only difference would be that they'd sell it to *everybody*, instead of there being a monopoly.'

Isn't that better?

'I don't think so. And even if it is, it's better still to destroy all of it.'

And you think that your personal judgement should decide

which way things go.

'If I had that beamer it damned well would.'

Then, since you haven't, it obviously follows logically that Bayon's way is the way that things should be done.

'Oh, be quiet! You're only arguing for the sake of it. You don't like it any more than I do. Your precious host's in mortal danger, remember. You ought to be worried.'

I am, he assured me, I really am.

He shut up and I eventually dozed off into a light and fitful sleep.

I couldn't have been asleep for very long, because there was still nothing happening when I awoke. Tob and Harl had changed places with Bayon and Ezra—the latter were now sleeping— but that was all. The atmosphere was steeped in silence and stillness. It felt like the early hours of the morning.

I contemplated trying to snatch the beamer, but Bayon had wrapped himself all around it before going to sleep, and there was no chance of disentangling it, quite apart from the fact that Tob was in the way. Instead, I decided to sound out Tob on the subject of demands and possibilities. I wasn't sure what kind of influence he might have with Bayon, but he seemed the likeliest ally I might find.

'What do you think Bayon intends to do?' I asked him, in a low whisper.

'I don't know,' he replied.

'Do you think he does?'

Tob shrugged. 'He's sleeping now. Won't be too strung out in the morning. We'll find out then.'

'Do you really think there's something to be gained by holding Krist for ransom?'

'There's none of us with any reason to love Krist,' he pointed out. 'In some ways, he's the linchpin of the whole system. He talks loudest and he's careful who talks back to him. He don't encourage much in the way of argument. There's a good many of us would like to deal out some punishment to Krist. Normally it wouldn't be a good idea, but with everything happening at once, I don't know that we might not get away with it.'

'Getting away with it is fine,' I said. 'But if you were willing to settle for less you'd have a damn sight better chance.'

'If we made a habit of running away,' he said, 'we'd all be at the bottom of the hotshafts by now. We want to get out of here. But it is our world, just the same as it's Krist's and my daughter's.'

'Daughter?'

'We didn't appear out of nowhere. We all got families.'

'Do you want to take your families with you when you go?'

'They don't want to come. They can't want to come, without being forced into our way of seeing things.'

'Surely they don't join in with this crazy farce of not seeing you or recognising that you exist?'

He shrugged fatalistically. 'Most do. It's their way of life. Some of them can bring themselves to remember, now and again. We can always get help if we need it badly. But once in a while and all the time are two different things.'

'But they couldn't want to stay here,' I protested. 'Not if they could go to a better world.'

He looked at me steadily, with an expression of patient long-suffering. 'Do you think we'd want to go if we could stay here?' he asked.

I don't know why it surprised me. This was, after all, *his* world—the only word he'd ever known. He'd never seen sunlight and he wasn't particularly keen to make its acquaintance. He probably wouldn't like it. It would cause him a great deal of physical discomfort, at first. And there was the change in sensory balance. Going native works both ways. I don't suppose he liked the thought of coming out of the warren any better than I would have liked staying there for good. It was purely and simply that life there was being made impossible for him. The symbolic non-existence worked both ways as well. By denying that the outcasts existed, the Churchmen actually robbed them of a great deal of that existence.

And all that could be put down to Krist. He was not solely

responsible, nor could he really be said to be at fault—he was trapped in the system just as the outcasts were. The fact that he was content with it didn't make him any the less trapped. But he was the Hierarch. He had to carry the can for anything rotten within his state. He had to bear the brunt of any grudges.

And Bayon's outcasts certainly had a big grudge.

It was no wonder that they wanted more out of Krist than for him to turn his back while they sneaked away to an alien existence. I could have been very sympathetic, if I hadn't been so dangerously involved.

'It's a dangerous game,' I said.

'So it is,' agreed Tob laconically.

'And you don't really know what you're trying to win, do you?'

'Maybe not'

'You can't stay here—no matter what you do.'

'I know that.'

'Isn't it better, then, just to make a clean break and leave the whole foul mess behind, to look after itself?'

'I got a daughter is part of that foul mess,' he reminded me.

'Have you? Is she really your daughter, now?'

'They can't make *that* any different.'

'But it is different, isn't it?' I didn't wait for him to answer. 'You can't possibly do her any good by making a stand here and putting on a big show. If anything, it will do her harm. There might be recriminations, whether you exist officially or not. You'd be doing her all the favours you could simply by slipping out quietly. Leave her to her life. You can only hurt her by forcing the Church—and her—to admit that you exist. There's nothing to be gained.'

He was silent for a few moments, and I judged that I must be gaining ground. The fact that a man has never run away in his life isn't sufficient reason for his making a stand at every crisis. There has to be something else to give him a reason for fighting.

'Bayon's the boss,' he said.

'You don't owe him anything. You follow because he leads.

You don't have to go with him, if he goes the wrong way. You aren't attached to him.'

'I don't reckon this is a good time to start betraying him,' he said.

'It has to be done, if needs must.'

'Not now.'

I didn't try to press him any harder. I'd said what I could. There was no need to hammer it home. Tob was as capable of thinking it out as I was. I thought that I could trust him to make a rational decision. I hoped that rational decision would be the same as mine. If it was the same as Bayon's, the future might be very bleak indeed.

We had been very quiet while we talked, but we had awaked Rion Mavra. As Tob retired slightly to resume his sentry position, Mavra came up behind me and knelt down. I turned around, and sat back against the tunnel wall.

'I'm worried,' he said.

'You're not alone,' I assured him.

'Exactly what power do you have with these people?'

'You saw him turn the gun on me. What do you think?'

'But he will listen to you. You can talk to him, at least. He won't hear what we have to say.'

'That's understandable,' I said, 'since you wouldn't even concede that he exists. You can't really expect to be able to argue him around to your point of view. What's the change of heart for, anyway? I thought you were aligned with the rest of them so far as voluntary blindness goes?'

'I'd be a fool if I refused to see a gun that wanted to shoot me.'

'There are a lot of fools in these parts.'

'Even Krist might compromise when it comes to facing a bullet.'

'Well, I hope so. Bayon probably won't settle for anything less. Somebody's going to have to talk to him eventually, and say some things he wants to hear. Somebody right at the top. I don't think you qualify.'

'I'd be easier to deal with than Jad Gimli. I warn you—Gimli might be intransigent. He wouldn't shed many tears over Akim Krist's death after the events of the last few days. I arrived late but I gather that a great deal of heat was generated between the two.'

'It's no good your angling for release,' I told him. 'Bayon won't consider it. He knows full well that it's Gimli we have to talk to. I don't know how much influence you've managed to win back since Titus Charlot imported you to act as his agent, but you're not going to convince Bayon or me that you can swing the council. What you can do, though, if you want to be co-operative, is tell me what you know about the stuff in the grotto. How much of it has got out?'

He spread his arms wide. 'I don't know. How can I? Nobody would admit to having removed any. The official story is that it's all there, but I don't know what to believe.'

'But there's a chance that if we can destroy the grotto we can exterminate the whole thing?'

'You can't destroy the grotto. And even if you did, it would only precipitate trouble. We'd be no better off.'

'We'd have sidestepped the issue of price. Bayon couldn't sell what he hasn't got, and he can't object to the Church selling it, either. It would make things a lot simpler from our side. And a lot of people might thank us for it, if they ever found out.'

'And if we were still alive to be thanked.'

'We'll have to overlook that, for now. If I can get the beamer away from Bayon, will you help me? I don't suppose Krist will help, but you might persuade Capra. If Harl and Ezra could be taken by surprise....'

'You're asking too much. There are four of them and three of us. They have the guns.'

'We could try.'

'No.'

And who could blame him? I didn't think much of it myself. As a plan of action, it was a joke.

It became redundant anyway, within a matter of minutes.

One of Bayon's men arrived at a run, and awoke Bayon and Ezra.

'They broke through,' he said, loudly enough to awake everyone else. 'They knew just where to hit. They've cut us off completely. We're sealed in. Arne's dead.'

Bayon was still shaking himself into full alertness but he missed none of the rapid speech. He didn't waste any time in wondering what to do, either. His contingency plans were already made.

'Harl! Get out into the tunnels and warn the rest. Bring them all back down here. Haul a couple of ore trucks back and barricade the tunnel just this side of the slit. We can defend there.'

Harl rushed off to carry out the orders.

'Anybody else hurt?' Bayon asked the bearer of bad news.

'Lud was hit. I don't know how bad. The others are bringing him back at his own pace. We had to leave Arne's body at the cutting.'

'How many were there?'

'I don't know. Eight or ten, maybe. They knew where we'd be and what to do about it. There was nothing we could do, Bayon.'

'All right. Nobody's blaming you. If we're shut in, we're shut in. It makes no difference, except that we've got a dead man to think about.'

I came to Bayon's shoulder.

'I think they've conceded the fact that you exist,' I told him.

'Don't you believe it,' he said. 'You wait until Jad Gimli comes down to the barricade.'

'You think he'll come? After killing one of your men and sealing you in? Surely he wouldn't dare. He'll try to starve you out. And he can do it, too.'

Bayon shook his head. 'He'll come. To talk to you. He's a lot more worried about the cave than about us.'

'Don't bet on that. He might already have his bit stashed away. It might serve his purposes very well to see the worms—and Akim Krist as well—burned up.'

'We'll find out,' he said confidently. 'Gimli will come.'

He was right. Gimli came.

CHAPTER FOURTEEN

Jad Gimli was a tall man with a hawk-nose. He was the whitest man I'd seen on Rhapsody. He was obviously proud of his provenance. He had grown his hair long and combed it back so that it swept away from his deep forehead and down to a point a couple of inches below his collar. His eyes were very pale and sharp, and his mouth very thin. He was impressive, by virtue of the fact that his etiolation had gone beyond the colourlessness which characterised most of the people of Rhapsody and taken on a boldness of its own. The whole effect was reminiscent of Angelina. But she was beautiful, and Gimli was hideous.

He waited on the outside of the barricade which had been formed by angling two ore trucks into an outward-facing V. I stepped across to join him. Bayon got up on top of the barricade and looked down on the two of us. Gimli didn't look up at him.

'What do you want?' he asked, his voice sounding distinctly viperish.

'Bayon holds the grotto,' I said. It didn't prompt a denial. Gimli simply waited. I continued. 'The outcasts hold Akim Krist. There are three other people in the tunnel as well—Rion Mavra, Cyolus Capra and a girl named Angelina.'

'Have you injured any of these people?' asked Gimli.

'No.'

'Then what do you want?'

'We want safe conduct out of the warren. For me and for all of Bayon's men. And we want the price of the grotto—whatever you have agreed with either Charlot or the man from Star

Cross.'

'And we want you to tell the whole world who took the price'. This from Bayon. Gimli gave no sign that he had heard.

'The council has not yet reached a decision,' said Gimli. 'We waited until we could hear what you had to say. You are Titus Charlot's pilot, are you not?'

'At the moment,' I said, 'I'm Bayon Alpart's spokesman. You know Bayon Alpart, I presume.' I pointed up at the man who towered over us. This time, Gimli did look up. But he gave no sign of recognition.

'Why did you take the grotto?' he demanded.

'Because it was valuable,' I told him, rather sharply. I had the feeling that he was trying not to communicate. I had expected it, but I wanted it out of the way as soon as possible. Once we were prepared to deal with the realities of the situation, then we could achieve something. Until then, it was all hot air.

'You imagined that you could steal the contents?' he followed through.

'We could have stolen some of it,' I pointed out. 'But Bayon wanted it all. He wants the full price. Whatever you care to ask of New Alexandria or of Star Cross must go to him, and we must all leave the world in order to be able to enjoy it. You can go back to exactly where you were before the grotto was discovered.'

'Except,' added Bayon, 'that you have a public renunciation to make.'

'We could take back the grotto,' said Gimli.

'Krist and the others would be killed.'

'So would you,' he said. 'You would gain nothing.'

'Quite so,' I countered. 'Give us what we want and we will gain our price, you will gain one Hierarch.'

'Another Hierarch can be elected,' he said dourly.

'Is that the council speaking?' I asked. 'Or Jad Gimli?'

'You can gain nothing by killing Krist,' he persisted.

'Nor can you.'

There was a temporary halt while we stared at one another

and contemplated the deadlock. Bayon jumped down from the truck. He rammed the power rifle into Gimli's stomach and forced the Churchman back against the wall. Gimli flinched, more because of the dirt adhering to the rock surface than because of the gun in his belly. He pulled himself back to his full height, but Bayon topped him by a good two inches.

'Who am I?' said Bayon roughly.

Gimli—perhaps wisely—did not attempt to deny that someone had a gun in his gut. 'I don't know,' he said—not very calmly.

'You remember me,' growled Bayon.

'I don't know you,' insisted Gimli.

'Well, hear me anyhow. I want my freedom. I want my price. And I want my peace of mind. Before I go, you'll tell the people of Rhapsody that Bayon Alpart is not dead. He exists. He lives. And he is escaping this world for a better one. He has found his own Exclusive Reward.'

'I'll tell the council what you say,' he said.

'Good. But there's one more thing before you go. Tell me my name'

'I don't know you,' said Gimli.

'Grainger,' hissed Bayon. 'Tell him what my name is.'

'His name is Alpart,' I said. 'Bayon Alpart.'

'That's right,' said Bayon. 'Now. *Tell me my name.*'

'You know your name,' said Gimli, between tight lips. My heart fluttered. I expected to see his abdomen disappear in a great gout of smoke and a big stink.

'Say it!' shouted Bayon. He thrust his face closer to Gimli's, and pushed harder with the barrel of the gun. But his finger didn't tighten on the trigger. He was determined to make the Churchman back down. He didn't want to kill him.

Seconds of agonised silence dragged by. Then Gimli decided that eventually compromise was inevitable.

'Bayon Alpart,' he said hesitantly, but not faintly.

'Thank you,' I said gently. 'Now you can tell the council who it is you have to deal with. I'm sure they'll have the same kind of difficulty which you have. But I'm equally sure that you can make them see what they have to see.'

Bayon took away the gun and stepped back. Gimli staggered off the wall, then collected himself together and set about dusting the filth from his shoulders.

'Never mind that,' I said. 'Go back to the council. Try to make them see our point of view.'

He turned his back, without a word, and walked away.

'We should send Mavra and Angelina with him,' I told Bayon. 'They're both prepared to acknowledge you. They could help us.'

'Who knows what Mavra might say once he's free?' said Bayon scornfully.

'You can't doubt Angelina. She's never denied you.'

'Angelina doesn't count. The council won't hear her. Gimli knows how things stand. He can tell the council, behind closed doors. They can make a real decision.'

'And what will that be?'

'They'll agree.'

'You can't believe that.'

'Then you tell me,' he said. 'What will they do?'

'Nothing,' I said. 'For the time being, they'll do absolutely nothing. Why should they? Time is on their side. They'll make you sweat.'

'It won't change a thing,' he said. 'I'm not going to back down.'

'I know that,' I said glumly.

'They'll have to do something eventually.'

'I know that, too.'

'They'll agree,' he said again.

'I only hope you're right'

I wandered back down the tunnel, and went into the grotto to have a look at the most valuable worms in the galaxy. Considering that it was supposed to be a cakewalk, I reflected, this trip was causing me a great deal of heartache. I wished yet again that I'd had the sense to stay in jail. The escape had been

Johnny's fault. It simply wasn't fair that it should be me who reaped the harvest of trouble.

If you were prepared to unbend a little, offered the wind, I could go a long way towards helping you get out of this mess.

'I'm sure you could,' I replied. 'But I would rather it was me that emerged from my sea of troubles, and not someone else.'

You look at things from a point of view which is both illogical and uninformed.

'So you keep telling me. Exactly how would you propose to extract me from my present predicament? Would we grow wings and fly, or grow spades and dig?'

We would need only the body and the mind which is already at our disposal. It would simply function more efficiently.

'I'm afraid this is a one-mind body. It wouldn't function very well for anyone else. I may not be much, but it knows me well.'

You're being deliberately ridiculous.

'You noticed.'

Only a fool refuses help when he needs it.

'Maybe so. But I don't think that my need is so great just yet. Come the day that I'm staring down Bayon's gun barrel and his hand is tightening on the trigger I just *might* decide that assistance is necessary. Even then I may elect to do my own superhero act. I'm certain that your offer is backed by the best of intentions, but I'm simply not interested. I'm sorry if this makes your stay here less than pleasant, but I didn't invite you into my mind. You picked me, you have to put up with me.'

Fine. But inside, you're still scared. What it comes down to is that you're more scared of me than you are of Rhapsody and all its terrors.

'That seems to be a fair way of putting it'

You belong on a world like Rhapsody. Grainger, the man without a name, without a human identity. The man alone. You do your utmost to preserve your isolation, just like the cavemen. Grainger alone against the worlds, always taking a course which no one else has chosen. You can't even justify yourself except in terms of compulsion and inner need. Why not admit to being a member of the human race? Why not admit that you'd *still* be a member of the human race if you allowed yourself to fuse minds with me? It's not so difficult, you know. There are people who've been human all their lives. They even profess to like it. And there are people with symbiotes like me. *They* profess to liking it, as well.

He gave up again, in apparent disgust. I was beginning to be heartily sick of his nagging. It was worse than being married. He hadn't been too hard to get along with at one time, when he first settled in. But ever since those few bleak moments in the Drift when he'd assumed command of my faculties, he'd been demanding complete emancipation. He made my head ache. He also made me even more determined that I wasn't going to give an inch. For a good many years I'd been getting myself out of trouble. I wasn't so old and feeble that I needed a nursemaid yet.

I sat down in the centre of the grotto, to wait. There didn't seem to be much else to do but wait. Ezra came in to take some water from the pool, and I assumed that he intended to use it for making some soup. That, at least, was a moderately pleasant thought. Bayon didn't seem to have had the time to let us all eat while we were busy playing at being bandits and making impossible demands of Jad Gimli.

A few moments later, Angelina came into the cave. The restrictions must be relaxing. Probably, the outcasts were inclined to be tolerant towards Angelina because she had never made an effort to participate in the invisibility game.

She looked tired, but interested in what was going on.

'How did you get on with Gimli?' she asked.

'Not well. We took the toughest possible line. You'd be in a better position than I would be to guess how he might react.'

She stretched herself, painfully. A stone floor is a bad place to sleep unless you get a certain amount of practice. She had obviously inherited the usual quota of aches. But she didn't seem to resent the fact that she was being held captive.

'Gimli will get rid of the problem,' she said.

'Mavra seemed to think that kidnapping Krist might sway

the council to his point of view.'

'Mavra's tongue runs away with him,' she said. 'Half of what he says is only froth. If he'd ever learned to be careful what he said, we'd never have been expelled to Attalus.'

'What did you do?' I asked, following the digression gladly.

'Heresy, of course,' she replied. 'Nothing serious. Just talk. But when they decide to have an accusation of heresy around here they try to bundle as many people into it as they can. That way, they reckon that it won't happen so often. The people here are naturally unfriendly and they mostly keep their ideas— heretical and otherwise—to themselves. But Mavra is a compulsive communicator. He talks to whoever will listen. Capra and Coria and the others were just unfortunate. They probably did no more than nod their heads in the wrong places. It was a very boring trial. They weren't at all keen to kick us out—they worry a lot about the declining population, and they couldn't really spare three young females. Two young females and Mavra's wife, to be exact. They were fairly pleased to see us back again. We could probably have hopped any ship that was passing this way during the last year, but we weren't to know what sort of a welcome we'd get.'

'You talk a lot yourself,' I commented.

'I'm a *real* heretic,' she boasted.

'You picked up some ideas on Attalus, then?'

'I had ideas,' she said levelly.

'What do you think Gimli will do?' I asked her.

'I told you. He'll get rid of the problem.'

'Sell the grotto to the highest bidder and leave it to them to collect?'

'Yes.'

'What about Akim Krist? And the rest of you, come to that.'

'It won't be his problem any more, will it?'

'Will the council sit still while he deals fast and loose with the Hierarch's life?' I asked.

'They're experts at looking the other way. Once it's not their grotto, it's not their problem, and it's not their responsibility.'

'Well,' I said, 'if you're right, they'd sure as hell better sell it to Charlot and not to Sampson. His solution is apt to be a great deal less direct. I only hope that they don't hold it against Charlot that his favourite slave is down here sitting on the pot of gold. If I get in his way, he's going to be extremely angry with me.'

'Can you blame him?' she commented. She sounded very much like my whispering companion.

'It's not my fault,' I protested, and then tried to change the subject. 'Whose side are you on? What do you want to see this treasure trove turned into?'

'I'm on everybody's side,' she said. 'This grotto doesn't belong to Gimli, or Krist, or to the council—and certainly not to you and Alpart. It belongs to the miners and the machine operators, and the refiners and the clerks.'

'That's a fine social conscience you have,' I said drily. 'But as of now the guns control the grotto, and will probably continue to do so. Unless, of course, the miners use *their* guns to assure a socialist redistribution of wealth.'

'They can't,' she said. 'They've spent all their lives here, in these caves, with this faith. They were born in the dark; they scuttle around in the dark. The faith won't permit them to bring the light they need down here. Light is a concession to weakness, and you need strength to win the Exclusive Reward. Light is always faint, because the voice of the Almighty, as reproduced by Akim Krist and his council, commands that the people should live in blackness, should work in blackness, should love and cherish blackness.

'The miners can't use their eyes any more. They're ashamed to lend any credence to their own senses. All that matters is the faith which they've been taught. Only the outcasts are thrown back on to their senses, because they've already lost the Exclusive Reward. Only the outcasts can see, and even they court darkness for their stealing and their skulking.'

'They live in a lighted cave,' I interposed.

'Do they? I'm glad for that, at least. But how bright is the light?'

'Dim,' I admitted.

'Exactly. Everyone here is four-fifths blind.'

'So you want to expel the darkness from Rhapsody?' I mused. 'That's almost as wild as Akim Krist's idea. Do you really think that you can re-educate the people? Do you imagine that replacing weak lights with strong ones will revitalise your whole society?'

'Life down here doesn't have to be the life of a worm,' she said. 'We don't want to come out into the sun. We don't want our air saturated with fog like the air of Attalus. But we don't have to make this world a pit of limitless darkness.'

'Maybe you do,' I said, 'if you want to receive your Exclusive Reward. Or have you given up believing in that?'

'I think this is our Exclusive Reward,' she said. 'If we choose it, then we certainly deserve it as our reward. And it's absolutely exclusive. There are no other worlds like this one, are there?'

'Not quite,' I conceded. 'This one is rather unique. But where did you get all these revolutionary thoughts from, if this culture is so very careful about the training of its children?'

'I used my senses,' she said.

'All by yourself?'

'Yes.'

'You didn't ever see the sun? You didn't read forbidden books? Nobody told you about the light?'

'No.'

'Well then,' I said. 'If it happened to you, it could have happened to a hundred others. The days of Rhapsody's darkness could be numbered.'

'Not while Akim Krist and Jad Gimli rule the council.'

'They won't rule for ever. All you need is one Rion Mavra, who talks too much because he thinks too much. And one Titus Charlot, to provide a link with New Alexandria. You could bring your light to Rhapsody, then.'

Bayon came into the grotto. The beamer was cradled in his arms like a baby. 'We eat,' he said. 'Outside.'

'How about you?' I asked him. 'Wouldn't you settle for an invasion of light to make this world move? Or are you only interested in your personal grudges?'

But he didn't know what I was talking about. He might even have thought I was being hypocritical. After all, the only reason I'd involved myself in the first place was in the hope of extracting a profit.

At that time, however, I didn't know what I wanted, and I could only wait and see how things were going to turn out.

CHAPTER FIFTEEN

It didn't take as long as I had feared. Not very many hours passed before Harl came to tell me that there was someone at the barricade who had expressed a desire to see me. I didn't bother guessing who it might be. I just went quickly down the tunnel to the barrier.

The conference had already started. Bayon was talking to Titus Charlot—on our side of the barricade—and he didn't look too happy. I hoped that Charlot hadn't annoyed Bayon too much. Gimli would hardly have given him a full account of how things stood down here, and Titus could easily make a mistake in handling Bayon which could result in the situation getting worse instead of better.

There were four of Bayon's men looking on with intense interest, including Tob. Harl came back just behind me, and I presumed that the others would be along as soon as they realised that things were moving again.

'Hello, Grainger,' said Charlot. He didn't seem to be bubbling over with goodwill towards me. I could tell that he resented whatever part I'd tried to play in the affair.

'Hello, Titus,' I replied. 'Have a nice stay in jail?'

'Uncomfortable,' he said. 'I'm sure that you've been having a much more exciting time of it.'

'Things have moved down here much faster than they would have up top,' I told him. 'But I wouldn't describe it as exciting, exactly.'

'And what do you think you're doing, *exactly*?' he said.

'Exploring the situation,' I said blandly.

'How did you get yourself involved with this bunch of cut-throats?'

That seemed a little undiplomatic to me, and I got the uncomfortable feeling that Gimli had given Charlot the impression that I was in command down here.

'The only casualty,' I pointed out, 'was on our side. If you could call it *our* side, that is. Bayon and I have our differences, and Bayon has the guns.'

'You're not trying to tell me that they took you prisoner along with Rion Mavra and the others?'

'Not quite,' I admitted, 'but a certain amount of tension has crept into our relationship.'

'So you're not in a position to demand your twenty thousand after all?'

'Would you have given it to me if I was?'

'No.'

'In that case, the matter is somewhat academic. I shall have to rely on Bayon's generosity, then. I take it that you've already told him what the council has decided.'

'Gimli was scared to come back,' interrupted Bayon. 'They sent this one instead.'

Charlot ignored him. 'The council did not send me. The council reached agreement some few hours ago that they would deal with New Alexandria over this matter of the grotto. The contents of the cave belong to me. The council has promised me full co-operation in any action which I care to take in order to seize my property.'

'Up to and including a pitched battle?' I asked.

'Up to and including the forcible recovery of the grotto.'

'It must be nice for Akim Krist to have so many loyal friends,' I said drily. 'And Mavra too—he was your friend, remember?'

'I came down here alone,' said Charlot patiently. 'I hope that there will be no need for violence of any kind. I am prepared to wait, if necessary. If there is any violence, it will be you who starts it.'

'Not me,' I reminded him. 'Bayon. He does exist, you know.'

'There should be no reason for the situation to degenerate to that extent,' said Charlot smoothly. 'I am prepared to be reasonable. What do you want?' The last sentence was addressed to Bayon.

'The price,' said Bayon.

'I'll pay any reasonable price,' Charlot assured him. 'What do you want?'

'I want the price that you paid to the council.'

'The arrangement which we came to is very complicated. In monetary terms, it would be difficult to calculate a matching figure.'

'I don't want an *equal* price,' said Bayon. 'I want *that* price'

Charlot returned his attention to me. 'What does he think he's playing at?' he asked.

'It's very simple,' I said. 'He has a grievance against the Church. He doesn't want the Church to benefit from the grotto affair. He wants to be paid their price, and he wants to withhold it from them. I'm afraid he has a somewhat nasty mind.'

'It must be the company he keeps,' said Charlot. 'It's out of the question, and you both know it'

'I know it,' I said, 'but...'

'The council isn't going to get away with shifting its troubles onto somebody else,' said Bayon doggedly. 'This business is between the council and me.' I saw the end of his gun twitch ominously. It looked rather as though Titus were about to join the party. But what could that possibly solve?

'Now wait a minute, Bayon,' I said. 'You can't go on just repeating your ultimatum. Can't you see that what happens here after you're gone just isn't that important? Charlot will pay you. The *Hooded Swan* will carry you all out of here. You heard him say that he isn't just going to pay the council a million or two and leave it at that. What New Alexandria has to offer is knowledge, not cash. Knowledge to help Rhapsody improve its own situation, to make things better here for everyone.'

'They don't want to make things better,' said Bayon. 'They

want to keep things the same. But I'm not going to let them do that. I'm going to crack their system. I want them to know that I exist.'

'You *can't*, Bayon. We just don't have that kind of leverage. Akim Krist isn't enough. The grotto itself isn't enough. There's *no way*, Bayon. You'll only get us all killed. What will it prove?'

'We can't die, remember,' he said. 'We don't exist.'

'That's their story,' I reminded him. 'If you wanted that way out, you could have killed yourself any time. You're behaving like a suicide, not like a survivor. This compulsive insistence on making them kill you is a concession to their way of thinking. You're trying to make them prove that you don't exist, by literally wiping yourselves out of existence. This is their game you're playing, not yours.'

The gun muzzle came up.

'Get back to the workface,' he said flatly. 'Both of you. We'll send Capra back with another message.'

'Do you want Sampson down here?' I protested. 'Sampson and his guns?'

'Sampson will pay my price. He won't risk his own life to kill us. He'll side with me, because I hold the grotto. He'll do things my way.'

'He won't.'

'Get back to the face.'

'Tob!' I appealed. 'It's your life as well. And all the rest of you. He's playing with your lives. Can't you make him see reason?'

'Shut up, *outworlder*!' said Bayon. Which just about said it all. No, they couldn't make him see reason. He was their leader. I was a suntanned, dark-haired starman. Charlot's hair was white, but there was no mistaking on which side of the fence he stood.

We were escorted back to the grotto. Harl made as though to push us onto the face with the rest of the prisoners, but Charlot stepped into the cave instead. Harl hesitated, so I followed Charlot. Harl apparently decided that it didn't matter much.

Bayon was following and, to judge by the sound of his voice, he didn't much care either. I could hear him directing his instructions to Cyolus Capra. I wondered vaguely whether Capra had decided to hear him or not. If not, I didn't suppose he would hold out for long. Akim Krist might die rather than speak a single word, but Capra would compromise without much of a fight.

'Well,' I said to Titus. 'This is it.'

'You should have let me talk to him,' said Charlot.

'You didn't even know how things stood,' I pointed out. 'I'll bet Jad Gimli didn't even tell you his name, did he? He sent you down here blind to make what you could of the mess, didn't he?'

'There was no reason for you to lose your temper,' insisted Charlot.

'I didn't lose my temper. You've got nothing to complain about. You'd have got not an inch further for all your oil and slickness. You just can't talk to the man. He's decided on his pound of flesh and he'll take no substitutes. If every ducat were ten thousand ducats, he'd have his bond. That's the way it is.'

'He's mad.'

'He's not mad. Just single-minded. He's been condemned to hell by these people and he wants them to let him out again and say they're sorry. He doesn't just want to run away. That's all it is.'

'You approve?'

'Hardly. It's likely to cost me my life. I'll do anything I can to change his mind. But I understand how he feels. I only hope he'll compromise when Sampson lets him down.'

'*If* Sampson lets him down.'

'You don't think he'd agree? Take on a whole planet?'

'I think he'll be very tempted to cheat. You saw him—don't you think he's an unsuitable vessel to fill with trust?'

'He's a hothead. But he's not stupid. He wouldn't dare side with fifteen men against a world.'

'That's not what I'm afraid of,' said Charlot quietly. 'When I said "cheat" I meant both ways. He'll promise everybody anything, and take it all himself. He'll have us killed and blame it on Bayon. He'll scuttle Bayon just as soon as he's off-planet with the goods.'

'He couldn't.'

'Let Well Alone,' Charlot reminded me. 'It's not even against the Law.'

'Well, all I can say,' I said, 'is that you have a very nasty mind. You really think it will go that way?'

'It's a possibility.'

'You'll never convince Bayon.'

'No.'

'We could warn him, though.'

'Would it do any good?'

'It might,' I said. But I had my doubts.

Things looked blacker with every hour that went by, and with every thought that crossed my mind.

A few minutes of unhappy silence passed, and then I said: 'If we could get the beamer away from Bayon, we could destroy the grotto in a matter of minutes.'

'And what would that prove?'

'No grotto, no price.'

'And then we get killed for nothing.'

'You mean to exploit this thing, if you win?'

He raised an eyebrow. 'Of course,' he said. 'What else?'

'You could destroy it. Why turn something like this loose in the galaxy? You know what it is, don't you? You've seen the worms—you know what they can do.'

'I hadn't seen the worms before I came in here,' he said. He was standing at the edge of the cleared area, and I saw that he was holding a dendrite—presumably an infected dendrite—in his hand. I hadn't seen him pick it up, so he must have been holding it since we first came in.

'In that case,' I said, 'there might not be any, except here. It can be destroyed. We don't have to take it back.'

'Grainger,' he said calmly, 'I'm too old and too wise to believe that you really care about the ethics of this situation. I suppose that your suggestion merely reflects your ever-present nihilism. But I'll explain it to you anyway. You'd be an idiot if you seriously thought that something could be blotted out of existence. Once a thing is known, it can't be unknown again. Forgotten, perhaps, but even that is only temporary. Everything which was once known will be remembered, in time.'

'There's only one cave full of these worms,' I said. 'They're a unique and contained life-system. All it needs is a power gun and ten minutes.'

'The life-system exists,' said Charlot patiently, ignoring the interruption. 'It *is*, and not all your justice or your strength or your courage can erase it. There's no question of whether the organism should be *allowed* to exist or not. It is, and it will be. There's an end to it. It's inevitable.

'This is a world full of people. Can you really believe that the wealth is just sitting here, abandoned? Can you believe that Jad Gimli hasn't got some little metal trees carefully hidden in some dark corner? Can you believe the same of Krist, and all the other council members? And what about the man who carried the bad news to Attalus and perhaps beyond? Almost every pocket on this planet might contain enough worms to breed millions more in a few days.

'You've got the entire problem out of perspective, Grainger. The fabric of this problem isn't woven from the cloth of ethics and humanity. The only point at issue is who is going to put money into the thing and who is going to make money out of it. That's all. Just that.

'There can be no control over when and where the weapon is employed. No one has that kind of power. Once a thing exists, it can be obtained. Anyone with the right price can have some. It may sound cruelly cynical, but I'm not quoting New Alexandrian principles, I'm quoting the state of the universe. Even if you were right, and not a single worm existed outside this cave, it wouldn't make the slightest bit of difference. If there's one thing that New Alexandria has proved beyond doubt it is that the important thing is *knowledge*. All that it needs is the knowledge that such a thing can exist, how and where. There are a million worlds like this one where the drills can start hammering their way into every sealed cave the echo detectors can find. There are a thousand laboratories which could establish an artificial environment and provide sequined thermosynths and cupro-carbon trees. Even without that, the cupro-carbon-chain destroyer would have been designed sooner or later. Everything which *can* exist *will*. Existence isn't the point at issue. All that matters is money, and the directions in which it flows. Nothing can change that. Certainly not one little man with a ray gun. You can't do anything to hurt the human race, or save the human race, Grainger. You're not big enough. Nobody is. Look after yourself, my child. Even New Alexandria can do no more than serve its own purposes. Nothing we can do could not be done without us. The only alternative to our way of doing things is somebody else's way of doing things. The only thing that anyone stands to gain on that scale is his name in the history books instead of another man's. My name will be in that history, Grainger, written as strongly as I can write it. You'd be far better employed working with me than against me. All the credit is mine, of course, but you might get a subsidiary mention.'

'I don't want a mention in your damned histories,' I said. 'You're that kind of lunatic, but I'm not.'

He shrugged his shoulders. The retort was irrelevant to the argument, and we both knew it. What he said was true. Nasty, but true. He was right about the synthetic nature of my ethics, as well. It had been nihilism, just as he'd said. If in doubt, kill it. But the laws of nature are just not designed to accommodate the negative point of view. Whatever will be, will be. That's life.

Quite, interposed the wind.

He said nothing else. He obviously thought that I'd said it all for him. But there was still to be no backing down. I had my own way to go.

'So you see,' said Charlot, eventually, 'there wasn't much point in your destroying the *Lost Star* cargo, either. It was only a gesture. It couldn't do any good.'

'What cargo?' I asked, with blatantly false innocence.

'What reason?' he countered. 'It can't have done you any good.'

That almost restored my self-confidence. (I wasn't likely to be without it long, in any case.) I had destroyed the *Lost Star* cargo, and the Khor-monsa had destroyed Myastrid. That secret still held, and might hold forever. Perhaps, in time, the Khor-monsa might manage to unknow what they wanted to forget.

Bayon came into the grotto. He was waving the beamer in a horribly suggestive manner.

'Capra came back,' he said. There was a peculiar edge to his voice. Things still didn't seem to be wholly to his satisfaction.

'He didn't waste any time,' I commented. 'What's the word?'

Bayon obviously thought that actions speak louder than words. He raised the gun.

'Wait a minute, Bayon,' I said hurriedly. 'Let's talk about it first.,

'There's nothing to say,' he said.

'There are things I want to say,' I assured him.

'Well?'

'Don't you owe me something? I came down here to help you. I've done what I can to get you what you want.'

'I don't owe you anything,' he said. 'You've done nothing.'

'I talked to Gimli for you.'

'You gave Gimli an excuse not to see me.'

'Now, come on,' I protested. 'Who wanted a mouth-piece? You *asked* me to act for you. I did what you wanted.'

'You didn't do enough.'

'Well, what do you *want* me to do?'

'I want my price.' He looked sideways, at Charlot. I shut up. It wasn't my argument, from here on. Bayon had made his point abundantly clear. Charlot had to give him what he wanted, or we'd be killed. Sampson must have agreed instantly to whatever offer Capra had taken to him.

'No,' said Charlot steadily. He didn't even seem to be worried.

'You can't...,' I began, and faded out.

'What you ask,' said Charlot to Bayon, 'is impossible. You know that as well as I do. You know that whatever Sampson might say, the Star Cross Company is in no better position than I am to grant what you ask. You're being carried away on an emotional tide—you've let your reason desert you. You not only ask that I should help you and not help the council and the people of Rhapsody, you also demand that I should try to humiliate the council by telling them what you have done and making them acknowledge it. This is ridiculous. You know that they cannot agree. They have already reached the limit of what they can do while remaining true to their situation. What you are trying to do is to force them to kill you. You don't *want* to get off Rhapsody. You're a coward. You're afraid of the opportunity, to escape—you're afraid that you might fail that opportunity. You've been trying to pick a fight ever since you moved in on the grotto. You want a blazing gun battle—a confrontation which will let you release all of your anger and your frustration and your hatred. It's so much safer than trying to start all over again.'

'I could have fought the council any time,' said Bayon.

'Alone? You need those men behind you, Bayon, because you're a coward. You had to trap them along with you, so that they'd have no option but to fight. These men are *hard* men—survivors. You'd never have led them into a suicide attack on the council or the miners. You're not like them, Bayon. You're one of the seventy-five percent, not one of the twenty-five. You're a diver, Bayon. A runaway. The only escape you can envisage is death. But you're not the kind of man to go alone, are you? You need company. You need moral support. Because you're a coward.'

I had to admire Bayon's patience. Most men I know would have cut Charlot in half while he was less than halfway through. But Bayon waited. Not because he conceded the truth of what Charlot was saying—far from it—but because he was letting the fury build up inside him. He was a slow man to anger, and he needed to be angry. Because, as Titus Charlot had said, he was a coward. He was afraid of what would happen if he pressed that trigger. He needed to be provoked. If Charlot had not provoked him, he would have had to provoke himself.

I glided slowly sideways, putting distance between myself and Charlot. If he fired at Charlot first, I would have a chance to go for the gun.

But he saw me moving, and the gun whipped sideways to cover me again. He took a half-step backward, so that his bulk was blocking the entrance to the grotto. He had to crouch in order to fit into the gap, but he seemed easy on his feet, and I didn't suppose he'd miss if I rushed him.

'Calm down, Bayon,' I said. 'Just think about it for a while. There's no hurry. Tomorrow or the day after will do. Sampson will wait. Just think about what you're doing. Talk to your men. We'll do all that we can to help you. There's no point in shooting anybody. You'll get nothing from Sampson. He'll cheat you— can't you see that? He's in it to maximise his profit. You're outcasts who don't even exist. He'll kill you, Bayon. We're your only real chance. If you kill us you kill yourself.'

I paused for breath. I was running out of things to say.

'You don't understand,' I said. 'You don't know what you're doing.'

'Well enough,' he said. He raised the gun to his shoulder and squinted down the barrel. He was aiming smack between my eyes.

'I helped you,' I cried, in panic. 'I'm your *friend*. Doesn't that mean anything to you?'

'About as much as it does to you,' he said, and fired.

I leaped sideways, and I hurtled across the cleared square. I cannoned into Charlot and took him down with me behind a rock at the edge of the square. The thermosynthetic carpet cushioned our fall, but I was stabbed painfully by several of the dendrites.

Two things saved our lives. The first was the fact that Bayon was not a practised gunman. No doubt he'd fired the beamer before, but he hadn't really come to terms with a weapon. He pulled the trigger just once, like a rife trigger, flicking the beam on and off again instead of pouring out the energy in a constant stream and following our dive. He aimed too high, as well, and the shot was quite harmless.

So far as *we* were concerned.

The second thing which saved us was that as I saw the trigger pressed I shut my eyes. Charlot's eyes shut reflexively when I barged into him. It wasn't just a blink. Fear closed our eyes tight and held them closed just long enough.

The beam was on high power and low spread. It made impact on the wall over an area the size of a thumbnail. It burned the organism clean away, of course. But not before it had raised the temperature of that tiny patch through hundreds of degrees to its flashpoint. A little bit of heat makes a hell of a lot of light. And the reaction time of the thermosynth was next to nothing.

Bayon was still sighting down the barrel. His open eyes were directed at the exact spot where the beam hit. The blast burned his optic nerves out instantaneously.

He screamed and dropped the gun.

When I stood up again, after the flash, he was rocking gently in his half-crouch, with his hands over his eyes. As I realised what had happened, and why, he staggered forward into the grotto. He fell to his knees beside the gun.

I ran towards it.

Tob was already in the doorway, with his rifle levelled. He must have caught the edge of the flash out in the corridor, because he didn't seem to be seeing too well. But he'd obviously been facing the other way. He wasn't blind.

'Don't pick it up,' he said, as I stooped and reached out my hand.

'You heard what went on, Tob,' I said. Another time, I might have grabbed it anyway and taken my chances. But I was off balance too. Not because I'd been dazzled, but because I'd been pushed. It was only just beginning to register that when I'd dived to avoid the beam I'd dived faster and harder than I'd intended.

As though I'd been picked up and thrown across the cave.

'You bastard,' I murmured. Nobody heard me except Bayon, who was only inches away. I think he took the abuse personally. But I wasn't talking to him at all.

Tob kept the gun level. But he had heard what went on. He might not be prepared to admit that everything Charlot had said was true, but he knew enough not to go Bayon's way.

'All right,' he said. 'We'll do it your way.'

I picked up the beamer. It was in my hands at last. I looked around at the glittering walls of the treasure cave. There must be a good many more worms now, following the big flash. I contemplated shutting my eyes and blasting away, exterminating the whole foul breed. But what Charlot had said had made that course of action seem somewhat ridiculous.

And besides, Tob might have shot me by mistake.

Tob came into the grotto to pick up his blind ex-leader. Bayon hadn't let out a peep since the scream. He had folded up completely, and looked more dead than alive. But when Tob picked him up, he was able to stand and be guided out of the cave.

I turned to Charlot. 'You damned near got us killed there,' I said. 'And you criticised me for losing my temper. What the hell did you think you were doing?'

He shrugged. 'He was going to shoot us anyway. Why be dishonest?'

I looked at him in amazement. 'You really are mad,' I said. 'However slim the chances, you could have agreed to his terms. Tell him anything. All you had to do was say yes instead of no.'

'He would have killed us anyway.'

'Just suppose,' I said, 'that you might have been wrong. You could have got us killed for nothing.'

'Not for nothing,' he said, as if it made a difference. 'For telling the truth.'

'Look,' I said. 'We're still outnumbered fifteen to two. If they decide that Bayon had the right idea after all, try a different line, hey? As a favour to us both.'

He didn't bother to reply. Nor did he bother to thank me for diving into him. I hadn't actually saved him, of course, but the thought had been there.

He just brushed his clothing free from the bits of crushed carpet which had attached themselves to him when we fell. And then he directed his whole attention to examining his prize.

I turned my back on him and stooped to pluck a handful of the dendrites. Two were infected, and I put them carefully into my pocket. Not wishing to be obvious, I wandered around aimlessly for a few moments before appropriating a couple more. Then, discreetly, I withdrew.

When Charlot went to get help from Nick, Johnny and the miners, I went to find Matthew Sampson. I wanted to make a deal before anyone else did.

I might still get my twenty thousand, if I was really lucky.

CHAPTER SIXTEEN

You're wrong, he said.

'*You pushed me*. I felt it. You were lying all along when you said that you couldn't influence my body without my consent.'

That's not what I said. I said that I couldn't assume control over any part of your body that was under your control. I did not interfere in any way with any part of you which you already control.

I finally saw the catch. 'You mean that you can control things that I can't?'

Naturally. It stands to reason that if I can assume control of your voluntary faculties when you allow me to, then I can also control such faculties as you have which are not under voluntary control.

'You can modify my reflexes. You can exercise control over my autonomic nervous system.'

Only insofar as you could yourself if you knew how and were prepared to learn. You are remarkably wasteful of the potentialities of your body.

'I don't want you exercising the potentialities of my body! I don't care how wasteful I am. It's my body and I'll use it as I please. Just because I don't concern myself with such party tricks as everting my gut doesn't mean to say that I want you to learn it for me.'

Why would I want to evert your gut? I'm not playing tricks, Grainger; I'm helping you to become a more efficient human being. How do you think you managed to keep going for so long when you were lost in the caves, without even feeling tired? You accused me of knocking you out, but I didn't. All I did was stop supporting your metabolism to relieve your need for sleep. Is that harming you or robbing you of your beloved independence? And when you say I pushed you—I didn't do that either. All that I did was adjust your nerves and your muscles so that you could move faster and farther than you could otherwise have done. I didn't do anything to you, I just put more of your own abilities at your disposal.

'And you intend to go on doing that?'

Of course. What's the point of letting you get tired when you want to stay awake? What's the point of letting you take ineffective evasive action when you could be effective? What's the point in my sitting back and letting you fail when I can help you succeed? I know you don't take a blind bit of notice of any advice I give you, but I can at least let you do things your own way efficiently. There'd be no sense in my just sitting here like a vegetable.

'Can't you get it into your head—your mind, I mean—that *I don't want any help*? I'd rather be inefficient my own way. I don't want to be a superman.'

I'm not making you into a superman. I'm just making you into an efficient *man*.

'I want to be *my own* man.'

But you *are*!

'Leave my metabolism alone.'

Grow up, Grainger. You're behaving like an idiot. What I can do to help you is no different at all from what your clothing does, or what physical fitness does. You have a body and it works. Why do you want it to work badly? Would you be better off if your reflexes were too slow to enable you to fly a ship? If your legs were too weak to let you walk?

'I only want to live by my own efforts.'

And you can. I can't stop you. Anything you can do, I can't. I can only let you do it a little bit better. You've got to live with it. If you continue in your present vein, you'll go completely insane. At least accept the realities.

I couldn't argue with him. I had no argument to use. That was the moment when the inevitability and totality of our association finally came home to me. It was late, I know, but I always had a lot of resistance to ideas I didn't want to accept. I don't think it was a turning point in my career as a host. I didn't change direction. He was still an unwelcome tenant. But while he was there he was what he was, and there was no use in fighting it. If rape is inevitable, as Confucius is reputed to have advised, lie back and enjoy it.

That argument took place in the caves, in Rhapsody's insistent darkness. At the end of three days, we were back in the sky, in company with the stars, and light had been let back into our lives.

I wasn't in great shape after the physical hardship I'd endured in the warren, but the wind's help as regards my involuntary faculties extended to fast healing. My hands recovered from their skinning sufficiently for me to lift the *Swan* and I was thus saved from the humiliation of taking the passenger seat while Eve flew the bird.

I was very careful, and we made transfer at the first attempt. I found a good, fast groove with no difficulty, and slid us into it as soon as humanly possible. Then I settled back and left the *Swan* to take care of herself.

'You should have let me lift her,' said Eve.

'Not on your life,' I said. It didn't need explaining.

We were alone in the control room. Charlot and Nick were down below nursing our ever-so-precious-cargo. Charlot was worried sick despite all his precautions. The worms were sealed in lightless containers, and had never been touched by human hand. Even so, the project looked unsafe. But Charlot was no fool, and if the worms could be saved, he would save them.

'You must have had a very bad time down there in the caves,' she said. We hadn't had a lot of opportunity to talk while Charlot was clearing things up on Rhapsody, and this was the first real chance she'd had to voice her concern.

'It's a hell of a place to get lost,' I told her. 'But once back into the daylight, all that darkness just fades away like so much nightmare. It hardly seems real, now that I'm back where I belong.'

'You haven't seen any real daylight yet,' she reminded me.

'The stars are all I need to reassure me,' I said. 'Maybe we ought to bring the passengers up for a look at the universe.'

'You want fifteen cave-men in your control room?'

'Hardly. I didn't mean it literally. It wouldn't do Bayon any good, in any case. He won't ever see the universe. He'll be in the black caves of Rhapsody for the rest of his fife.'

'I was surprised that you brought him along,' she said. 'He tried to kill you.'

'Charlot's decision,' I pointed out. 'I only work here. But we couldn't leave him on Rhapsody. They couldn't do anything with him. He has to stay with Tob and the rest, because no one else can know that he exists.'

I'd offered Angelina a free ride to wherever she wanted to go, as well as the outcasts. But she'd elected to stay behind, and support Mavra for Hierarch. I didn't fancy their chances much. Akim Krist might be old but he was tough. He'd last for years.

'Besides,' I added, 'they were all different down in the caves. With darkness in the way that they lived their lives, in their voices and in their eyes. They'll be different men altogether once they're on a different world. Perhaps they can change Bayon, too.'

'You sound almost sympathetic,' she said. 'It doesn't really become you.'

I shrugged. 'I was down there a long time. You don't understand what it was like.'

'I was down there too. In jail.'

'A prison is a prison,' I told her. 'It isn't life.'

'I thought you'd forgotten all about it,' she said.

'Sure,' I said. 'It's splitting up and dissolving. I can look back and wonder how I ever got to be involved in it. Its logic is becoming illusory. Reason aren't reasons any more. Give me a day or two and it will be all cancelled out. Dead.'

But I was wrong. I was only trying to forget. I never really did.

But all this is retrospective. The story really ended where I made it begin: down in the caves, in darkness....

CHAPTER 17

In a dark covert, within the capital but beyond the feeble gleam of the apologetic city lights, I finally ran Sampson down. He'd not been easy to find. He was unpopular and had barely survived an extended stay in the city jail. He was just about to leave, to face the inevitable wrath of his superiors.

'You almost got us killed,' I told him.

'It was no part of my plan,' he assured me. 'I just agreed to Alpart's terms to try to cut myself back in. I didn't know what he had planned for you. I swear it'

'OK,' I said, not much interested in his protests. 'I didn't run down to start a fight. I've got some of the worms. If you want them, the price is twenty thousand.'

He didn't leap for joy. It was dark, so I couldn't see his expression, but I was getting used to darkness. I could tell that he wasn't interested. He was tired.

'You're a little late, Grainger,' he said.

'Somebody else had a secret stash,' I said—I'd been half expecting it. 'You already got supplied.'

'Something like that,' he said. 'I've had offers from more than one source. I set up deals, too. But there's more to it than that. When I say you're late, I mean you're *late*. I guess nobody told you the bad news?'

I put my hand in my pocket and fingered the coppery dendrites. It had, of course, been far too good to be true. I just couldn't be carrying a fortune in my pocket. No chance. Charlot hadn't attempted to stop anyone stealing from the grotto. He'd acted as if it simply didn't matter.

It obviously didn't.

'All right,' I said, sounding as tired as he did. 'What's the catch?'

'That stuff's been locked in a stone coffin for millions of years,' he said. 'It's a bit much to expect that you can go barging into a set-up like that and not upset things somewhat. They were lucky, I suppose, not to have destroyed the whole thing before they found out what it was.

'But there's more to a life-system than heat and light, as you damn well know. The ringworms are half-and-half organisms. They're walking a physiological tightrope. Each one is as sensitive and as delicate as hell. And not just to heat and light and air. Each worm is a protocoenocyte and each one manifests one hell of an allergy problem. They sensitise to human proteins and human-associated proteins in a matter of minutes. They don't turn bright green or writhe in agony, or anything like that, but those worms you have in your pocket have a probable life-span of a couple of days. No matter how many times they divide in the meantime.

'You don't have to believe me, of course. But we ran a check on board the ramrod the moment Gimli gave us the first consignment. Your boss knows as well—he's down in the grotto right now with four-foot forceps and as much sterile equipment as he can raise or improvise. You've been out of touch while you were catching up with your beauty sleep.

'You were right, you know. We should all have stayed in jail. The kid and I only stayed free for a matter of minutes anyhow.'

I took the dendrites out of my pocket and held them in the palms of my hands. I couldn't see the worms. I was feeling a mite sick, but I'd never really believed that it was going to come off.

'The others felt just as bad,' Sampson assured me, as if it helped. 'Gimli lost his fortune too, and one or two of the others.'

'Great,' I said. 'Just great.'

'You can't win them all,' he said.

'No,' I agreed, 'but it would be nice to win one now and again.'

He laughed drily, and then he was gone, leaving me alone in the shadow.

I shivered.

ABOUT THE AUTHOR

Brian Stableford was born in Yorkshire in 1948. He taught at the University of Reading for several years, but is now a full-time writer. He has written many science-fiction and fantasy novels, including *The Empire of Fear, The Werewolves of London, Year Zero, The Curse of the Coral Bride, The Stones of Camelot,* and *Prelude to Eternity.* Collections of his short stories include a long series of *Tales of the Biotech Revolution,* and such idiosyncratic items as *Sheena and Other Gothic Tales* and *The Innsmouth Heritage and Other Sequels.* He has written numerous nonfiction books, including *Scientific Romance in Britain, 1890-1950; Glorious Perversity: The Decline and Fall of Literary Decadence; Science Fact and Science Fiction: An Encyclopedia;* and *The Devil's Party: A Brief History of Satanic Abuse.* He has contributed hundreds of biographical and critical articles to reference books, and has also translated numerous novels from the French language, including books by Paul Féval, Albert Robida, Maurice Renard, and J. H. Rosny the Elder.